Extended Clip

Lock Down Publications and Ca$h Presents
Extended Clip
A Novel by *Trai'Quan*

Extended Clip

Lock Down Publications
P.O. Box 944
Stockbridge, Ga 30281

Copyright 2020 by Trai'Quan
Extended Clip

Lock Down Publications
Like our page on Facebook: Lock Down Publications @
www.facebook.com/lockdownpublications.ldp
Cover design and layout by: **Dynasty Cover Me**
Book interior design by: **Shawn Walker**

Stay Connected with Us!

Text **LOCKDOWN** to 22828 to stay up-to-date with new releases, sneak peaks, contests and more…

Thank you!

Submission Guideline.

DISCARD

Submit the first three chapters of your completed manuscript to ldpsubmissions@gmail.com, subject line: Your book's title. The manuscript must be in a .doc file and sent as an attachment. Document should be in Times New Roman, double spaced and in size 12 font. Also, provide your synopsis and full contact information. If sending multiple submissions, they must each be in a separate email.

Have a story but no way to send it electronically? You can still submit to LDP/Ca$h Presents. Send in the first three chapters, written or typed, of your completed manuscript to:

LDP: Submissions Dept
P.O. Box 944
Stockbridge, Ga 30281

DO NOT send original manuscript. Must be a duplicate.

Provide your synopsis and a cover letter containing your full contact information.

Thanks for considering LDP and Ca$h Presents.

Trai'Quan

Prologue

Flash.... Flash.... Pause.....

-Backwards-

The third 9mm slug exited his chest and his body jerked while the second slug exited, only to be followed by the first. All three slugs traveled the short distance back into the barrel of the gun. The holes in his chest closed themselves, after all of the blood went back into his body.

Flash.... Flash.... Pause.....

His eyes regained their focus. He watched as the fire went back into the gun. He got a brief look at the face of his assassin, then he took a step back and closed the door.

Flash.... Flash... Pause......

He stood in front of the door. But glanced back to where the Taurus .45 lay on the coffee table. Then looked back to the door again. He walked backwards until he reached the sofa and re-sat. His hand reached out and the cigarette butt jumped out of the ash tray into his hand. He watched as the smoke came down out of the ceiling and went back into the butt. The ashes went from gray, back to fire red, then turned brown. It became white and extended longer. He saw the smoke come out of the air, form a circle, then turn back into plain smoke as it went back into his mouth. He brought the cigarette back to his lips and seemed to spit the smoke back into the butt of the cigarette.

Flash..... Flash.... Pause.....

He sat down in a daze.....

He heard the knock at the door. And everything stopped.....

"Look through my eyes and see what I see, do as I do and be what I be, walk in my shoes and hurt yo feet. Ain't nowhere to hide, I lurk in the street.... Burnin in hell, but don't deserve to be, got niggas I don't even

know, who wanna murder me......"
-DMX

Some people think that you have to be made bad, taught wrong, shown how to be something other than what you are. In some cases, this is true. But some people simply transform. They morph into another phase of that which had already lay dormant inside. Once unleashed, it's extremely hard to control, which is why some simply let nature take its course.......

Chapter One

-2001-

It was four days before his 21st birthday and Chalice wasn't even feeling like a grown man. With the sun out as bright as it was, the day was turning out to be a hot one as he sat outside on the green box, along with Que and John-John. All three of them were sipping from the double duce bottles they held and smoking cigarettes.

"Ayo Sun.... Yo mom dukes gone let you throw a party fo' yo b-day?" Que asked. He had a deep New York accent because he was originally from Queens and hadn't been in Augusta no more than two years.

"Nah, I doubt it," Chalice replied. "A nigga really too old for that shit."

Out of the three, Chalice was the only one originally from Augusta. John-John and his family had moved there from Alabama and none of them looked alike. Where Que was a brown skinned brother, around 6'1 and about 192 lbs., John-John was light skinned and only 5'9, with more weight on him than he should've had. He looked like a shorter version of Heavy D, the rapper. Chalice was 6'3 and 215lbs, which was perfectly cut, since he had been boxing at the Augusta's boxing club. Something he'd been good at the past six and a half years. With his shirt off, Chalice didn't look like a boxer, he looked more like a body builder and he was dark skinned, with very wavy hair.

Taking a moment, Chalice took a pull off the cigarette. The beer was just about flat and Chalice was actually thinking about tossing it to the ground. He would've said something about going to get more, but then the candy apple red, Silverado 1500, extended cab pulled up across the street from where they sat.

"There go that nigga Paint," John-John said.

"Yeah, a nigga sho' wouldn't mind painting his ass," Que stated.

Everyone knew Paint's history. The fact that his sister was the one who put him on as the rumor went. Erica's ex-husband had been killed in the game five and a half years ago. Some kind of deal gone bad or something, but Erica was left holding the dope.

They watched as Leslie open the door and let Paint in. Then the door closed as John-John looked at his cheap watch. "Damn, yo. I'm about to dip. Y'all know I've got to be at work early in the morning," he said.

"Kick rocks then nigga," Que replied.

Chalice remained quiet. It was a good thing he worked at night. In fact, he would have to be at the circle K gas station at 11: o'clock tonight.

Que sold dope and could care less about a job. Besides, he'd been convicted of a felony and it was hard as hell to get a white person to give you a job. Hell, even the blacks who owned their own business wouldn't give a felon a job.

"Shit, you'll be going in too ain't you?" Que asked.

Chalice turned up the beer. Then before he spoke, he pulled out another cigarette. "I go in at 11. But you ain't about to chump me off about my job. So you can save it nigga," Chalice told him as he lit the cigarette.

Que smiled as he turned his bottle up. He liked Chalice. He didn't exactly know why, he just did. Chalice was a straight up nigga and he didn't bite his tongue either.

It was 10:30 by the time Chalice went into the apartment. Pam was sitting on the couch talking on the phone and from what he could tell, she was talking to Erica.

"What's up lady?" Chalice asked.

Pam looked up at her son. "Boy ain't you supposed to be at work?"

Chalice didn't pay her any attention as he proceeded upstairs so that he could get ready for work. He didn't hear whoever it was saying something to Pam, nor when Pam spoke back to them. But by the time he reached his room, Pam called out to him.

"Erica wants to know if you're still going to be chasing her once you turn legal," she said.

"Tell Erica don't play wit' grown people, before she end up getting it for real." He waited. Then heard Pam laugh.

*** *** *** *** ***

Erica was so fed up with Paint's bullshit. Lately, since he'd been messing with that bitch Leslie, he'd been coming up short on her money. She really didn't have the patience to be dealing with it. She'd been sitting inside of her den after getting off the phone with Pam. Pumpkin was asleep, she had to go to school in the morning.

Erica sighed. Her mind told her to call Antwan, who was the nigga she'd been messing with lately. But for some reason, even that thought didn't seem appealing to her too much these days. The nigga was only a toy to her and Erica needed a real nigga in her life. Someone who could really hold things down.

Her mind drifted to Chalice, Pam's son. His birthday was in four more days. She laughed. Erica had been teasing Chalice for years now, about giving him some when he turned 21. But then she thought, *"I wonder if the nigga took it seriously."*

Chalice made it more than clear that he was interested in her. Erica knew she didn't look 35. She was, as she thought, fine. At 5'11 and 158lbs., Erica had a 35-26-41 figure, with a pecan tan complexion. She also had short length hair and large, sexy, oval shape eyes.

She pictured Chalice who had a very nice build. He wore his hair cut in a clean fade with the waves up top and that little diamond stud that he wore in his nose was too

10

cute. For a minute she nearly lost herself in thought but then her current problems resurfaced. As of now, she held a little more than 8 kilos of Peruvian Cocaine and then there was the club she owned, 'Black Lace', which was a strip club. In fact, it was one of the four in this area.

When Erica moved to Augusta, she'd began to like the city quickly, mostly because there was a lot of money in it. With the club, plus the fact that she'd been getting dancers from both Miami and Atlanta to come, she was making more money than she would have back home.

Pumpkins daddy had died, or rather been killed and Erica was the only one that knew about the cocaine he had. The guy that killed him was now locked up in Florida. There had been some type of altercation in one of the clubs and Delow had beaten the guy pretty badly. The guy had left and Delow, thinking it was over, went back to enjoying himself. A few hours later, when the club was about to close and everyone was leaving, Delow had a bit of a walk since he had parked his BMW 7351 at the far end of the parking lot, but then he wasn't expecting any trouble

When he pulled out his keys to unlock the door, another car pulled up beside him with the window already down. The .45 came out of the window spitting flames four times. Delow's body jerked and danced all four times. When he fell, the guy stepped out of the car and put two more bullets into him.

The news was harder on Pumpkin, she'd been nearly ten at the time. That had been almost six years ago. Delow had left her with four kilos of Peruvian Cocaine, which he'd been getting from a Columbian named Joker. The same Columbian she dealt with to this day. Inside his safe she'd found $825,000.00, of which she put $400,000.00 into the 'Black Lace'. Erica wanted to have the nicest strip club in Augusta and it was. Then she used the other 425 grand to get established in Augusta. She bought a home in a nice area and the Range Rover that she drove.

Erica had met Pam late one night at Kroger's. They were both standing in line, about to buy whatever, she couldn't actually remember what. But a conversation started and before either realized it, phone numbers were swapped. That had been four years ago, now Pam was her best friend and the manager at her club.

Pam had always known that Chalice was interested in Erica and she told Erica that if he still had that interest when his 21st birthday came, then so be it. He'd be old enough to do whatever then, but Erica hadn't thought that his infatuation would go that far. It wasn't as if she didn't find him to be very attractive.

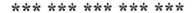

Paint sat at the kitchen table where he cut up the ounce he'd gotten from Erica earlier. She'd told him to bring her $1100.00 back off it. *"Shit! She'd be lucky if he brought her $900.00,"* Paint thought as he puffed on the cigarette that hung from his lips. He could remember when she used to let him get an ounce for $750.00. Now days she was on some other shit, talking about she wanted $1100.00. As if it was his fault the cops were running raids and one of his houses got hit. That raid put him back a good deal too. Then his sister started acting as if she couldn't feel him on that. She acted as if he were *trying* to get raided.

Then there was that nigga Antwan, who wasn't doing shit for her. All that nigga did was eat, fuck and sleep. At least Paint put in work for her, but nah, the bitch couldn't see that far. The only thing she understood was her money. If it hadn't been for that nigga getting killed, she wouldn't even have the shit. Now she acted as if she was worth a million bucks.

Paint looked up as Leslie stepped into the room. She

was still wearing the thigh length t-shirt that she'd been wearing for the past two days. He'd been meaning to tell her to put something else on, but the shit just left little for the imagination to explore and he couldn't lie, he did like watching her in the shit. At the moment his mind was focused on the dope and the fact that he was behind on his bills.

Paint thought about all of the pressure he'd been under lately. Because of the raid, his boys had been complaining about having to double the hustling. Also, he owed money on his car notes and the furniture in the apartment. What he really needed was a good lick. Something that would put him on his feet and that he could work from. The petty shit wasn't enough.

*** *** *** *** ***

Erica sat in her living room reading a book and relaxing.

"Ma, I'm going outside to chill wit' Tammy. A'ight?" Pumpkin asked.

Erica looked up and saw her daughter was wearing a pair of blue jeans with a solid blue halter top. She knew that this was the latest fashion for the teenagers in the streets. "Have that ass home by dinner time and don't be out there in no trouble!" She watched as Pumpkin hit the door like she might change her mind. Erica shook her head.

At only 15, Pumpkin thought that was grown. Especially since she had the body of a 23 year old, with wide hips and big thighs. The only thing on her that was small was her breasts and Erica knew that she was bound to have trouble out of her soon. It was a good thing that they had the type of relationship they had. She trusted Pumpkin to talk to her about anything. Especially sex.

Erica had turned her attention back to the book. In a way she'd been amazed at how the older woman in the book

13

was so into the younger man. Then she laughed to herself, she was in the same position herself.

*** *** *** *** ***

Chalice had been tired from last night he'd put in on the job, plus, he'd worked three extra hour's overtime. The girl who'd been scheduled to relieve him had been late for work. Her car had broken down and she lived so far away that she couldn't have walked. Instead, she called a cab and the cab had taken a whole hour and a half to get there, plus the drive was 15 minutes to the store. Chalice stayed an extra hour after she arrived because she hadn't even been in her uniform when she'd gotten there and had to go to the back and change.

His eyes' began to get heavy the moment his head hit the pillow. He'd taken a long shower and didn't have enough energy to even play around with Pam before she went to work. He began to drift off into la-la land, thinking about his favorite subject, Erica. It was funny in a way, because the closer he got to his birthday, the more his mind had been focused on her. Chalice knew that she'd still been talking to that nigga Antwan, but then again, Antwan wasn't really holding shit down. He had once overheard Erica telling Pam that she was getting fed up with the nigga's free loading shit. But at the same time, she did appreciate the attention he showed her. He just wasn't thug enough for her nature.

Chalice thought about that. If only he had a sure chance at getting with her. Antwan was 31, only four years younger than her. But it wasn't like being 14 years younger. Shit, he was almost six years older than Pumpkin.

As his thoughts faded, he fell into a deep dream, a dream of himself and Erica. One where he played out the roll he heard her tell Pam that Delow once had. Yeah,

Chalice thought, *"She ain't seen no real thug yet."*

*** *** *** *** ***

Paint pulled up to the projects where most of his workers trapped out of. He saw his niece Pumpkin and her friend standing near a dark blue Suburban, talking to that nigga Troop. Paint had never liked the nigga, mostly because his truck was of the latest model and had nice rims on it. The nigga thought he was all of that.

For a moment he started to go over and pull Pumpkin away from the nigga, but he knew that once Erica got wind of it, the nigga wouldn't even think about her again. Besides, he was on the way to make a drop and in if the nigga got fly, he wasn't in no shape to be fighting no nigga with an ounce on him. He'd made up his mind to get word to Erica about the nigga trying to talk to his niece though.

Troop saw Paint when he first pulled up. At first he thought the nigga was going to come over and run off at the lip. Especially with the way he looked over at them.

"Ayo Pumpkin. Ain't that yo broke ass uncle over there?" He asked.

Pumpkin looked up at the nigga with an evil expression on her face before she turned and waved at Paint. She already knew that not many people respected her uncle because they thought he was soft, working for her mother. Pumpkin sort of felt sorry for him. She could remember when she'd been young and Paint had been there for her when her mother had been out with her father. She knew all about her mother's past, she knew the story everybody else didn't. That her father had once been one of her mother's tricks, back when her mother worked in two strip clubs in Miami. Erica told her of the struggle she'd endured, but she knew that both her father and mother had endured much by her getting pregnant. They'd killed Erica's boss and gone

15

into a brief period of robberies. They'd done all of that while Erica was pregnant and eventually caught a break when they robbed a nigga for a half kilo of cocaine. That same half kilo that put her father on.

But her Uncle Paint had been there during those times when they were out hustling. Which was why, in a way, she felt sorry that he hadn't really come up yet. Then again, Pumpkin knew Paint was lazy and looking for that pie in the sky. She just hoped that he didn't run and tell her mother on her, but she knew he probably would.

"Nigga, what type of shit is this?"

Paint looked down at the nigga who sat at the table. Richard, AKA Rich nigga, or Rich, was his next in charge. But in a way, Rich acted as if he was the one really running shit.

"I told you, Erica is trippin because I lost out on that lil dope in the raid. So we gone have to rework shit, or find another nigga to buy work from. And you know them niggas round the way charging 15 to 1600 an ounce," he explained.

Rich just shook his head. "So where's the rest of it?" He asked.

"Shit, that's all of it," Paint explained as if he were the bitch and Rich the pimp.

"You..., never mind." Rich had to catch himself. "I don't see how you let Erica play you like you're the sucka. Nigga, bitches suck dick. Not real niggas. Fuck the raid, you her fucking blood, she should be giving you dope."

Paint knew that Rich never liked Erica any way. Mainly because she was a female and she had all the dope. Plus, he tried to get with her a while back but she turned his ass down after she laughed in his face.

"If I was you, I'd be thinking about taking that shit from her," Rich commented.

To that, Paint didn't reply. The thought had entered his

mind, but he also knew that Erica, even if she was a female, wasn't no soft female. And then there was that nigga Cujo. He pushed most of her major weight and the nigga acted like he was her father or some shit. Cujo was 56 years old. He stood around 6'4 and weighed a little over 260lbs, all solid. He had, maybe 12, young niggas who ran under him. Plus that nigga Red. But Cujo never took to the streets. He also ran security at the club.

Paint knew that to rob Erica he would probably have to kill her to get away with it. But, he also knew that she had at least four to five kilos on deck too and that was real tempting.

*** *** *** *** ***

Rugar sat watching the Circle K gas station for quite some time. Contemplating a strong armed robbery, he'd finally come up with a plan. He couldn't do it when the two bitches were working because there had been reports that at least one of them packed a .38 and was known to shoot. It couldn't be first shift either, because there were two men plus the owner there at that time. His best chance would have to be when the young nigga was there. He worked with another female, a white bitch and to top that, after five, the owner would be gone.

Rugar doubted that the nigga would have the nerve to pull out a pistol, not to mention the will or the skills to use it. Plus, he didn't believe that he carried one. And the white bitch was too busy trying to think and act black so a nigga would notice her stupid ass. But the bitch wasn't bad looking, Rugar thought, *"I wonder if the nigga done fucked the lil bitch yet?"*

He told himself that odds were eight to ten that he had. What sane nigga would turn down some free, all white, pussy?

Extended Clip

But that was neither here nor there. His mind went back to the Circle K. He guessed that the ticket would be about $1700.00 or better, just off one shift. Plus, by that time, traffic would be slowing down, which meant that he could be in and out before someone pulled in to get gas.

Yeah and it was a sweet lick too. Rugar finally made up his mind, he was going do it tonight! Since he knew tonight was the nigga's last night, he'd be off for two days and in his way of thinking, two days was a long wait.

Trai'Quan

Chapter Two

"It's a small world so you betta guard yo secrets. It's easy to get money but it's hard to keep it....."
-Jadakiss Kiss of Death

"So Pam, you gone come to the club tonight or not?" Erica asked. She'd been on the phone talking to Pam for the last 25 minutes and seeing as it was Pam's night off, Erica had asked her the same question several times.

"I might. But you know I'm trying to figure out what to give this nigga for his birthday tomorrow," Pam told her.

"Me!" Erica laughed. "Hell as much as he wants me, I guess he'd consider me a good gift. What do you think?" She asked.

Pam laughed too. "Girl be serious. You know that you're not about to be serious wit' him. Besides, ain't you already got a nigga you play around wit'?" She listen as Erica sighed, then huffed on the other end.

"Yeah, I guess you can put it like that. But seriously, I'm about to drop this nigga like a whole pack of cigarettes. And the sex ain't all that," Erica told her.

Pam kept quiet. She'd been thinking about something else that she was about to ask. "E', let me ask you something."

"What? Do the nigga got a big dick? Hells no!" Erica laughed.

"Nah girl, be serious. We can talk about the nigga's dick some other time." Pam joined her in laughter. "But fo' real. This is about Chalice."

"Okay. Now I'm serious," Erica said.

But Pam thought that it still sounded as if she were playing. "Well, I'm gone tell you straight up how I'm looking at the situation. Chalice really is infatuated wit' you and I believe that when tomorrow hits, he gone give yo ass the business...." She trailed off in thought.

"Come on wit' it girl. I was just about to get scared and hire a body guard," Erica stated.

"Girl, don't hurt that boy. You know he still young and you're old as dirt."

"And F... f... fuck you." Erica faked like she was stuttering, but she wasn't slow. She could see that Pam was serious about what she'd been saying. "Girl listen to me," Erica became serious as she spoke. "You're my best friend and I would never hurt that relationship. Besides, you know I'm lookin for a real, thug nigga. Chalice ain't even moving like that."

"Mm hmm.... And if he is?" Pam asked.

"Shit, then I might need to be the one being careful. Cause they ain't building niggas like that no more," Erica told her.

"I dunno girl. I put 23 chromosomes into that nigga myself. He might just surprise yo old ass." Pam laughed.

"Nah, quit playin. But fo real, would it bother you if we did hook up?" Erica asked.

Pam took a moment to think about it, but their conversation ended without her responding.

Just as she hung up the phone, Pumpkin came in through the front door. "Hi Ma, what's up?"

"You!" Erica snapped.

Pumpkin stopped dead in her tracks. *"Damn,"* she thought. *"Paint punk ass done snitched on me."* "....Uh, what's on your mind?" She asked as she sat down on the couch next to Erica.

"You know what I'm talking about boo. That old ass nigga Troop. That nigga ain't talkin bout shit and you know it."

"But it ain't even like that. We was just talking and hanging out," Pumpkin explained. "I mean he did try to get wit' me. But seriously...." She made a face. "Now if we were talking about Paris, that would be another subject altogether." Pumpkin said.

Erica shook her head. When Paint called her and dry snitched about Troop, she'd made a call to Cujo who said he would have a talk with the nigga. But Paris, who just happen to be Cujo's son, was a different subject indeed. For one, Erica like Paris. He wasn't like Troop, who was too old by nine years or more. Paris had just turned 18 and Cujo had him going to Augusta College, pushing the new 2002 Lincoln Navigator. Erica didn't have any problem with Paris.

"So let me ask you something, since we in a serious conversation," Erica said.

"Ah. I know you ain't about to ask me if I'm still a virgin again," Pumpkin responded causing Erica to laugh.

"Nah, that ain't it. Besides, that thang had better still be untouched. At least until you're 17."

They both laughed at that.

"Okay, I'll try not to give Paris none until after I turn 17."

"The question is about Chalice," Erica said and watched as a smile appeared on Pumpkin's face. Pumpkin already knew about that little teasing vibe between them. She'd even called Chalice Step Daddy a couple times as a joke and laughed when he tried to hide a blush.

"His birthday is tomorrow isn't it?" Pumpkin asked.

"Yes it is. Why?"

"So..., uh..., you gone stop playin games and stuff, you know...," Pumpkin insinuated.

"Hold up Miss Thang." Erica laughed. "What's that supposed to mean?"

That caused Pumpkin to laugh. "Well, look at it from my point of view. Even I can see y'all need to get something off your chests. No matter how hard you try to hide it," she explained.

Erica laughed at her. "So you ain't got no problem wit' the age thing?" Erica asked.

Pumpkin screwed her face up before she spoke. "Being honest, I'd rather you kick it wit Chalice and be happy than be wit' some fool that's gone free load off us. Like yo boy Antwan."

Erica gave serious thought to what she said and it didn't take her much to realize it was time. It would've been different if the nigga was hustling. "So you good wit' Chalice? But he ain't no hustler either." She said.

"Chalice might surprise you and he is fine," Pumpkin laughed.

Erica's hand shot out and hit her on the leg before she even realized it. Causing Pumpkin to laugh. "And just why are you looking anyway? I thought you were having dreams of Paris." Erica watched as Pumpkin held her head back and looked upwards.

"Yes, I know."

Together, they broke out laughing.

*** *** *** *** ***

Chalice's mind wasn't even on the question that Que had just asked. All he could remember was that it was some shit about a beer. They were walking towards Smiles gas station and Chalice was dressed in his uniform for work, but Que was wearing baggie jeans with a Hilfiger shirt. He only came along to kick it, since Chalice didn't have a whole lot of time. All Que did throughout the day was push dope for Cujo. So he had time to bullshit around.

"What was that?" Chalice asked.

"I said, are you gone let a nigga get a duce on the house? You know that dingy ass white girl ain't gone notice," Que explained. He was talking about stealing a double duce with Chalice's permission.

23

Extended Clip

"Nah nigga. That shit ain't cool. If you get it and the inventory comes up a certain way, I still gotta pay for the shit," Chalice told him. But in essence, his mind had been on thoughts of Erica lately. His birthday was tomorrow and he'd pretty much made his mind up. He was just hoping that she hadn't changed hers.

"Ah nigga…. Like two dollars and change gone hurt yo check," Que wined.

They were now a block away from the store and Chalice began, "You see…, its niggas like you that don't want to see other niggas wit' shit. You must've forgot you just told me that you got nearly a grand in yo pocket and that $400 of it is yours. But you want me to go in there and pull a stunt, when I don't make but $375 a fuckin week. Nigga, you make that shit in a fuckin hour but you can't respect a nigga trying to work for his," Chalice responded.

Que walked on for a minute, deep in his own thoughts. He was actually considering what Chalice had just said to him. "You know what?" He said as they stepped into Smiles' parking lot. "You right…, truth be told, I feel that shit. But yo, what you gone do when a nigga ain't got no job to fall back on?"

"Same shit." Chalice hunched his shoulders up and down. "Buy me some crack and put my hustle down. The only difference in me doing it and you doing it, is that I'm a make the shit legendary."

When they walked up to the door, Chalice could see the two niggas inside getting ready to leave. The white girl was also inside.

"Listen, I'm gone get this duce and get out of your way. But yo, you still going to the club tomorrow night?" Que asked.

"No doubt. That's how I'm gone bring in my 21st birthday," Chalice stated.

And they stepped into the store.

*** *** *** *** ***

For a minute, Pam thought about not going to the club. But then again, it had been a while since she'd gone out. Plus, it was work and she knew Cujo would be there. In fact, he was always there.

She smiled to herself as she removed the midnight blue dress from the closet. The dress itself came to her mid-thigh and was extremely form fitting. She knew that she had a nice figure for her age. At 39, she stood around 5'9 and weighed 136lbs with measurements of 34-24-39. Most of her weight was in her lower body. On top of all that, her skin complexion was dark and she had slightly slanted eyes, which in essence made her a beautiful woman.

Chalice also had her eyes. His were slanted and a light hazel in color. A lot of people assumed that they were brother and sister, instead of mother and son.

Pam laid the dress across her bed then went to the bathroom to take a shower.

*** *** *** *** ***

Rugar stood in the parking lot of TW Josey High school, across the street from the gas station. He brought the Newport that he was smoking up to his lips and inhaled. The car that he leaned against had been stolen earlier that day, from Sandersville GA. He knew it wouldn't hit the search list until maybe tomorrow, but it was already 7:30.

He had decided to pull the lick around 8:00, just before the 8:10 close, when they shut down long enough to count the money. This was done every night when they removed most of the money to put in the safe, in the office.

Since people who came to the store regularly already

knew this, traffic was light, which made it a really good time.

Chalice sat on the stool inside the store. He was behind the counter, keeping a close eye on Kelly as she checked the aisles. There were a few people left inside the store, but not many. As he sat there, Chalice had to admit, the white bitch was fine, for a white girl. She was around 5'6", maybe 115 to 120lbs and her ass wasn't flat either. She was sort of a cross between a red head and brunette, but she wasn't a bad looking chic.

Looking at her now forced him to think back to the last piece of pussy he had, which had been his ex-girlfriend Angie, who was about his age, maybe a year younger. They had broken up about a month ago and hadn't had sex in like six weeks. Shit just wasn't going good. Angie had a baby by another nigga and for some reason she couldn't leave the nigga alone. Half the time Chalice came around the nigga had been there. He tried his best to make it clear that he still had his own locks on her. After a while he simply became fed up with it. Plus he had the feeling that they were still fucking. Especially since after they broke up, she went now back with the nigga.

The store was now empty, as he had already cashed out the few people who'd been in there. Kelly was now busy straightening up some cigarettes that were in a display right in front of the counter and Chalice was so caught up in his memories that he was unaware of the nigga walking through the door, wearing the black hoodie.

Rugar could tell that he caught them slipping. The stocking he wore had been itching his face, so he hoped to pull this lick as fast as possible and get out. Since he hadn't looked at the nigga yet, he knew that they didn't know he wore a stocking. Using the element of surprise, he both reached out with one hand and grabbed the white girl as she began to stand and used his other hand to pull out the .357,

26

which he immediately put to her head.

"Alright nigga…, let's not play hero, cause I sure will make two or three big ass zero's in yo chest," Rugar stated. "Bitch, shut the fuck up!"

Kelly had begun to scream, having being caught off guard like that. But she quickly closed her mouth.

"Now, use one of them bags and put all the money in it as fast as you can. If I think you shitting on me…, pow!" Rugar told Chalice.

Although Chalice had been quiet the whole time, he wasn't stupid. This was, however, the first time he'd ever been robbed and the first time a gun had been pulled on someone near him. Still, he remained calm. He punched the buttons on the register to open it and then used one of the brown paper bags to put the money in. Every time he looked up he could tell that Kelly wasn't feeling the whole vibe, since the gun was pointed to her head.

"Come on nigga. You takin to fuckin long! And don't forget about the bag under the counter either. I want that too!" Rugar demanded.

Chalice didn't flinch. Instead, he reached under the counter and pulled out the money bag. He was about to open it and pull the money out but was interrupted.

"Nah, just set both bags on the counter and take five steps backwards. Then turn around and stand still. If you do anything other than that hero, I'm a put a couple hot ones in you."

Chalice did as he was told. After a while he heard the bag being picked up, then he heard Kelly squeal. He didn't try to turn around, nor did he try to look back.

"H…, he's gone. Hurry, call the police!"

He heard Kelly talking, but his mind was on something else. Chalice had been thinking that he didn't have a gun. He never had, because to him guns brought problems. Now, even without one, he saw that shit was bound to happen.

Extended Clip

The police finally came, but they didn't do too much. They asked a lot of questions and then had both of them sign a report. That was about it. They said that this was the first report they had of that gas station being robbed and since neither one of them saw the guy's face due to the stocking, there wasn't a whole lot they could do about finding him. There wasn't much else to go on, his back had even been to the main camera, so that didn't help either.

Both Chalice and Kelly were left shaken by the whole experience. Not so much him, as her. The way he saw it, nobody got shot. Still and yet, Chalice didn't desire to repeat the experience.

*** *** *** *** ***

Erica and Pam sat at their usual table, which was on the balcony, overlooking the center floor and the bar of the club. The music was nice, a little too loud, but it was a club.

Erica leaned over towards Pam, who had been sipping her drink. "Guess who keeps looking up here?"

"Who?" Pam asked as if she didn't know. She looked around the club and both of them began to laugh.

"Girl, you know you've got that nigga Cujo on the ropes," Erica laughed.

"Oh, him. I thought it was somebody else. Shhhhh, he's been lookin up here," Pam told her.

"Mmm hmm. But he ain't came up here yet. I wonder if it's got something to do with that dress you wearing. Got that old ass nigga's dick harder than blue steel...." Erica cracked and they both laughed.

While Erica was still laughing, Pam looked down and that's when she saw Antwan walk through the door, into the club. Using her left hand, she bumped Erica's arm repeatedly. "Girl look who just came in!" She exclaimed.

Erica pulled herself together so that she could look, but

when she saw who it was, her thoughts automatically turned to Chalice. Erica had been thinking about him since she'd talked to Pumpkin. She was thinking that it was about time to push this nigga.

Pam could tell that she had something on her mind now. "Girl, what up? You act as if you've just seen the ghost of Christmas past or something?"

But Erica didn't respond immediately. She watched as Antwan waved, then made his way over to the stairs.

"I think it's about time to let this nigga know."

Causing Pam to do a double take at her. "You fo' real. Girl, quit playing," Pam replied.

Antwan stepped into the box, speaking to both of them before he pulled out a chair next to Erica. He placed one hand on the back of hers and looked at her. "So, what's up baby? You alright?" He asked.

Erica looked at him then sighed. "Yeah..., I'm good. But this thing between me and you...," she paused a moment. "It ain't working."

Pam could see that this was about to be serious. Especially with the look on Antwan's face as Erica's words sunk in.

"Look girl, I'm about to go get a drink at the bar. I'll be back in a minute." Pam told her as she stood up. "I just hope 'you know who' don't hold me up too long."

As she left, Antwan being the nigga that he was, watched the way her hips moved in her dress, not realizing that Erica was watching him.

"Listen baby...," he began. "I know things ain't exactly peaches and cream, but a nigga workin on it."

Erica sipped her drink as she listen to him, but inside her mind the hustler was talking to her. That part of her that nobody really knew about. "Look Antwan..., it's over. Period! We just ain't built the same way," she firmly stated.

"Is this about me not hustling? Well, that's what I was

about to tell you. Baby I've changed my mind. I'm a do it," he somewhat pleaded.

But she sighed deeply again, this nigga just didn't seem to get it. Erica knew that it was the Georgia nigga in him. "You a nice guy and all that," she began to explain to him. "And we had some good times together. But the truth is..., there's always been something missing." She thought to herself, *'Like you're too soft.'* But she didn't say that out loud. She said, "Look Antwan, this just isn't meant to be. But there ain't no hard feelings. A'ight?"

"As if a nigga's emotions weren't involved," he mumbled. They sat a moment, thinking. "So I guess the next nigga gone be that nigga hu?" He asked. In his mind he knew that she was chumping him off. But he cursed himself because he realized that he should have taken those nine Oz's she tried to give him. How the hell he hadn't figured it out that a dope bitch would want a dope nigga. "So this is it huh? But I guess it's my fault. Because I didn't step up when I had the chance to. But it's all good." He paused then stood up. "I guess I'll be seeing you around.

Erica remained silent and emptied her drink. There was nothing else to say. The nigga just wasn't built like that. And then there was Chalice..., was he?

Trai'Quan

Chapter Three

"Through all of the possibilities, through all of the possibilities.... Sounds like a love song, sounds like a love song.... [Most incredible baby].... I can't see em coming down my eye, so I gotta make the song cry.... I can't see em coming down my eye, so I gotta make the song cry.... I know I seen em coming down your eye, so I gotta make the song cry....."
-Jay Z Song Cry

Rugar sat in the apartment he lived in with his mother. She'd been at work for the past four hours and now, as he sat at the kitchen table, he counted out the money he'd just robbed from the gas station. So far his count was $775 and there was still another stack of bills to count. However, the last one was smaller than the rest had been. From the looks of it, he'd say all together, it would be about nine hundred and change. Which was better than he expected.

With this money, he planned to go see Troop. Not many people knew that Troop was letting an ounce go for $750 to people he knew and that wasn't many people. With other niggas, he would jack the bid up to 900 or better. Depending on how good business was at that time.

Rugar himself had been visualizing a better tomorrow. But he hadn't had the funds to make it happen. The main rule in the streets is that 'to make money, you have to have money.' So now that he had money..., wasn't no stopping him.

*** *** *** *** ***

Hours Later.....
Chalice had been lying across the bed in of his room,

his mind in limbo. The robbery at the store kept playing over in his head and he realized that the job itself wasn't paying him enough to take those types of risks. What if that nigga had been on some type of dope? If he had gotten jumpy, he could've put a slug in Chalice for real. If he'd lived, he wouldn't have received anything from it. The cracker who owned the store wasn't even concerned with his health. He'd seen that with his own eyes. The owner had been called, but upon his arrival, he'd been more worried about Kelly and the money. He didn't even ask if Chalice was alright and if he had gotten killed, all it would have done was leave Pam in debt. But Erica would help.

Speaking of Erica, Chalice's mind wondered. He knew that Erica controlled a good amount of dope. Plus that soft ass nigga Antwan, wasn't trying to get on like that. He'd over heard her telling Pam how she tried to make the nigga. Now Chalice was wondering if Erica would put him on. Even if they didn't take this birthday thing seriously. Would she be willing to help him get on his feet in the game?

Then he thought about the $2800 he had on stash in his shoe box, in the closet. He had something to start with, he wouldn't have to step to her with his hand out. The thing was, if they did hook up, he'd be able to stand firm and show that it wasn't about her money.

Erica was fine, in fact she was beautiful and she had that sort of street, ghetto, business type personality. He knew that she was about her paper.

Chalice thought about Que and John-John taking him to her club tomorrow night. Then as an afterthought, *'Might as well use the $800 and buy something nice.'* Shit, it was his birthday. No telling what he could get. Usually, he rocked the blue jeans and T-shirt, with some sneakers, but as time went by, and thinking that at 21, a nigga should be growing up instead of down.

Yeah.... Chalice thought. *'I might just switch the game*

up and see what happens.' With those thoughts decided, he drifted off to sleep.

*** *** *** *** ***

When she opened the door and stepped into her house, the last thing Erica expected to see was Pumpkin, still up and on the phone.

"Ahem.... Do you know what time it is Miss Thang?" She asked as she placed her pocket book on the table and went into the kitchen. Since it was a Friday night she wasn't going to make an issue of it.

"Ma, Paris said what's up?" Pumpkin called out.

"Tell Paris if he wants to make sure you stay a good girl, he might think about letting you get some sleep," Erica stated and then listened as she heard them laugh.

The good thing about it was that she knew Paris had enough respect for her than to let Pumpkin do something stupid. But then again, he was still a nigga and his father was a street nigga.

Standing at the sink, drinking a glass of water. Her thoughts suddenly shifted to Chalice. She couldn't, for some reason, get that young nigga off her mind. Maybe, she told herself, it was the fact that his birthday was tomorrow. "And I still haven't gotten him anything for his birthday."

Mentally she contemplated what a good gift for a 21 year old nigga would be.

*** *** *** *** ***

Paint was too confused to speak. Rich had given him the rundown on a good plan. The whole thing sounded simple. He said that all they had to do was get Erica at one of the gas stations, or somewhere, then they would both run

34

up on her in ski masks, kidnap her and then make her take them to the dope.

But the more he thought about it the more he didn't like the plan. "Nope. That ain't gone work. Too many people gone see the shit when it goes down," Paint stated. "I've got a better idea. All we got to do is watch the crib. Since this morning is Saturday, Pumpkin won't be there tonight. She'll be at one of her friend's houses and more than likely, that nigga Antwan gone come over. So all we gotta do is give em a few minutes, then push up in the crib. You feel me?" Paint explained.

The whole time he spoke. Rich had been nodding his head. "Do she got a gun?" He asked.

"Yeah. But I doubt she'll have it out. She ain't been on no gangsta shit since Miami," Paint replied.

"Just in case…, I'm gone bring in this nigga I know. He good on this robbery shit and for a three way split on five keys. I know the nigga gone be down," Rich suggested.

"Man…, I dunno…, another nigga shit could be less than five keys," Paint told him.

Rich gave him an evil look, one he knew Paint didn't exactly catch. Dumb ass nigga. "Don't even worry about it," he replied.

*** *** *** *** ***

Saturday: The Birthday

Chalice, Que and John-John were all walking towards the mall. They had to walk since Que had his Ford Explorer in the shop. The truck was eight years old and had a million and one problems, but Que refuse to give up on it.

"Damn, you think a nigga gone be able to get wit' one of them strip club hoes?" John-John asked.

"If yo money right nigga, you can get with Mariah Carrie." Que laughed. "But wit yo job, nah, I doubt it," he added as he continued laughing.

Chalice laughed too and was just about to speak as they turned the corner of the street and saw two niggas there. One had his hands up in the air, while the other nigga had a 9mm in his hand. On the ground lay a whole lot of loose money and some jewelry.

The nigga with the gun turned and saw them. "What? Y'all niggas ain't never seen nobody get jacked before. Just be glad it ain't y'all!" The Jackboy spat.

"Shiiiiit.... Between the three of us," Que responded. "You might get five bucks, if that. You don't see niggas be walking instead of riding the bus?"

As he spoke, no one noticed that Chalice's eyes were stuck on the gun.

The Jackboy laughed. "Nah, it ain't worth it. But y'all had betta bounce before I decide to take that little bit too."

None of them spoke after that, they just kept walking passed the crime scene. Chalice noticed that the nigga being robbed had tears in his eyes. In a way, he felt bad for the nigga.

Two streets later, Chalice asked, "Que, nigga. What the fuck you joking wit a nigga like that for?"

Que laughed. "Ah nigga, I wasn't worried about that nigga. Shit, he ain't the only nigga out here wit a gun."

He watched as Que pulled his shirt up and showed the butt end of the 9mm that he had. "Shit. Maybe I should get me one of those. Niggas getting jacked for they shit in broad day light," Chalice stated.

Que looked over at his friend. He could sense that Chalice was serious, but he didn't understand why. "Yo nigga is you serious?" He asked.

"...Uh..., I'm thinkin bout it."

"Shit.... Guns done went up these days. I could get you a nice piece for about $400," Que explained as they walked. "You just let me know if you decide to cop one for real," he added.

At the mall, Chalice couldn't decide on the shirt that he wanted. The choice was between a Tommy Hilfiger blue 4XL, long sleeved joint, or the Phat Farm cream colored, pin stripe, long sleeve 4XL, pull-over shirt. One was $75 and the other was $97.

"Yo, if I was you, I'd be trying to save that loot and buy the cheap one. At least it's real," Que told him.

Chalice had already spent close to $300 on Timberlands and a nice pair of jeans. Either shirt would go with them. He'd also gotten some Perry Ellis cologne for men and the shit smelled good.

But his silent thoughts kept going back to the robbery in the streets. That was the second robbery in under three days. While he'd been working at the store, the gun had been aimed at Kelly as well. Then seeing the nigga with the tears in his eyes as he was being robbed, Chalice didn't really know what to think. He kept asking himself what he have done if the gun was aimed at him.

He replaced the Tommy and decided to spend the extra on the Phat Farm. You only live once he thought, there would come a time when he would be able to buy what he wanted. When money wouldn't be the issue.

*** *** *** *** ***

The phone ringing woke Erica from her sleep and before she even reached to answer it, she looked at the time on her watch. Damn! She couldn't believe she'd slept until 10:30.

"Hello," she answered.

"Damn girl. You sound as if you done had some good dick or something," Pam stated.

"Nah, I'm saving it for somebody special," Erica stretched.

"Special huh? And who might that be?"

"Damn you nosey. Ain't you got something else to worry about?" Erica replied.

"Mmm hmm... 21 today. I wonder what tonight gone look like?" Pam said.

Pam was joking. But at the same time Erica's mind wasn't. She seriously was thinking about hooking up with Chalice. "Anyway, what's up bitch? I know you didn't just call to worry about my coochie," Erica responded.

"Ain't nobody worried about yo nasty coochie," Pam laughed. "You just make sure you clean that thing before you give my baby some of it."

"Oh, and fuck you too. With a very big dick that is," Erica laughed.

"Anyway, I called to see if you was going to the club tonight," Pam told her.

"...Uh..., I thought so. Why, what's up?"

"Girl, you didn't hear it from me, but Chalice and his friends went to the mall. I overheard him talking about he wanted to impress somebody tonight," Pam reported.

"Impress?" Erica said.

"Said something about not wanting to look like a bum," Pam added.

"Mmm hmm. Knowing Chalice and wit' them niggas, he probably gone still wear jeans and a t-shirt. Mind you, they might be a different color."

Erica laughed and they talked about a few other things for a minute. Cujo, Pumpkin and Paris etc....

"Listen. Let me go ahead and get up, I've got a lot to do today. But I'll call you back in a few," Erica told her.

After they hung up Erica continued to lay in the bed for a moment thinking. She didn't have to really worry about what to wear tonight. Tonight she intended to wear the Teal green, body dress that she'd only worn once before, when she'd been on vacation in Miami. She knew the effects *that* dress had on niggas. She wasn't concerned with other niggas tonight. Her mind would be on one nigga...

Extended Clip

Chapter Four

The inside of the club was lavish, especially the construction of it. It was built in two levels, with a large opening on the right hand side of the door as you entered. Through the opening were stairs that led up to the VIP balconies, which looked sort of like sky boxes. In the direct center of the club there was a rotating bar, which moved in a full 360 degree circle. There were four bartenders that moved around to fill orders.

Since it was a strip club, there were a number of smaller stages around the main floor and a large stage next to the DJ's booth.

Since neither Chalice, Que nor John-John had ever been inside of a strip club, this was a new experience for all three of them.

"Let's get one of those tables near the big stage," Que said. "I heard that they take it all off up in this bitch. I wanna smell me some pussy!"

They made their way through the people and found an empty table. Both Que and John-John sat on the end and faced the stage, which left Chalice sitting behind them. There was a girl already up on the stage, dancing to the 'Thong' song and she was already naked, dancing on the pole directly in front of them.

"Whew! Yo, I'm about to go get us some drinks. It looks like we gone need em," Que said. He stood up and walked towards the bar.

Chalice had to admit, they did have some nice ladies up in here and he was about to say so when John-John, after looking around and seeing what the other men were doing, pulled out a roll of money and peeled off a bill. John-John was holding the roll of one dollar bills and waved one at the woman up on the stage. Chalice watched as first she looked back, then caught sight of the bill. Her eyes went next to the roll John-John was holding. Then she looked into his face and pointed to herself. John-John nodded and smiled as she came off the pole and made her way over to him.

The woman took the money, then squatted down right in front of John-John. Since he'd paid for the shot, her pussy was right in front of him. Moist and wet, looking like a big Georgia peach.

"Damn...," Que said as he came back to the table. "That nigga ain't even waste no time did he?"

Chalice laughed. But he took one of the three drinks and sipped it. John-John, by this time, had pulled off several more bills and was now talking. "What's yo name girl?" He asked.

"Fantasy. Why?" The girl replied as she continued to dance.

"Shit...," John-John licked his lips like he was the thirstiest nigga up in the joint. "What a nigga REALLY gotta do to see about some of that?"

They all watched as the girl smiled. "Daddy..., my kitty don't come cheap." She twisted her hips, then went back down to a squat once more. "What you got in mind big money?"

Chalice knew John-Johns' mind was in over time now, the roll he had in his hand looked like about $200. But he knew that John-John had also cashed his check, so he had at least a grand in his pocket.

"Nigga...," Que jumped in while John-John kept licking his lips. "You betta wait until you see some more bitches before you throw away yo money." Then he raised his glass and sipped from it.

Chalice on the other hand, had been watching the girl and he caught the evil look along with the word she mumbled under her breath.

"Hater...." Then she turned with an extra twist in her hips and strutted off while they all watched John-John's tongue hang half way out of his mouth.

Chalice suddenly began to receive funny vibes. Kind of like when Spiderman knew there was about to be some danger. He knew somebody was looking at him. When he turned and looked, he didn't see anyone. Mentally he was thinking about Erica because he knew that she and Pam were there. He just didn't know where.

"Okay.... I'm kinda feeling the casual thug look...," Erica said to Pam as she looked over the balcony at Chalice. Both she and Pam were sharing a private booth up on the balcony, which kind of made it easier for her to spot Chalice and his crew.

"Well, it ain't like he's rich," Pam stated. "The nigga work at a gas station."

"For now...," Erica added. But continued sipping her drink as they watched one of his friends get another dance.

"I sho hope that young nigga waving the money don't sleep wit' nothing," Erica said.

"Pishhhh..., who, John-John?" Pam turned her own drink up. "That nigga probably got a pack of condoms too."

They both laughed.

"You think he gone like my dress?" Erica asked.

When she pulled the dress out of the closet, Erica had known that it was form fitting, but she hadn't had it on in a while. Since then, she'd put on a pound or two and now the dress was smaller and hugged her body like a python.

They were both in the mist of laughing when one of the bar waitress' eased the door open and made her presence known.

"Oh..., what's up Megan?" Erica asked.

It was a good thing the club was adjusted to body temperature, because the white girl would have frozen to death otherwise.

"Ah... 'You know who' just asked me to see if Pam would like to visit his booth for a minute."

42

Pam looked at Erica and they both giggled. "And?" Erica asked.

"Well, I suppose I'll be..., uh..., leaving yo old ass up here by yo self."

"Don't count on it." Erica looked back at Megan. "Uh, Megan. Do you see that young man down there, sitting with the other two? The one wit' the Phat farm shirt on." The white girl looked, then nodded. "Well, I need you to bring him up here for me. Oh and don't tell him why. Just show him to the booth and that'll be all. Thanks."

As the white girl left, Pam looked over at Erica. They both broke out in laughter at the same time.

"Well, I guess I had better go see what the old man wants. Probably want some coochie." Pam laughed as she left the booth.

By this time, another dancer was on stage. Her name was Envy and she looked somewhat Mexican, with dark hair and green eyes. But she had the body of a sister. This time it was Que who'd been waving his money in the air. Chalice couldn't do anything but shake his head. He was about to get up and go buy the next round of drinks when the white girl tapped him on his shoulder.

"Excuse me. But I've been asked to come get you. If you don't mind, could you follow me?" She requested.

Both Que and John-John were looking as if they had gone out bad or something. "Damn, this nigga ain't wave a fuckin bill and he's got bitches coming at him," Que stated.

"Shiiit... They must know it's the nigga's birthday," John-John said as he smiled.

But Chalice didn't say anything. He only shook his head as he stood up and followed her. She walked over to the stairs and started up as Chalice followed behind her. Once at the top, she led him to a door and said, "Just go inside and someone will be with you in a minute." She stepped by him and actually brushed her ass up against him as she left.

'Well…,' Chalice thought. *'Must be one of the girls from the stage, but which one?'* He open the door and stepped inside. At first Chalice was confused. Then he was horny. Next he felt like he'd drank a fifth of Gin straight. Erica stood up and looked straight at him as Chalice thought, *'Damn this woman fine.'*

"Well, do I get a birthday hug from the birthday boy, or not?" She asked.

"Mmm hmm. Do Pumpkin know you stole her dress?" He asked.

Erica looked down and smiled. "What, this ole thang?"

"Yeah, that ole thang," he repeated. "Got me over here scared to touch you. Shit, what if you get pregnant?" He asked.

"Damn, all that from a hug?" Erica joked.

They found themselves embracing anyway. She even smiled as his hands moved down to squeeze her ass cheeks.

"Careful Romeo. Don't start no mess and it won't be none," she told him.

Chalice squeezed, just one more time, before he leaned back and looked down into her eyes. "Girl, I'm all about starting something. So what you wanna do?" He asked her.

While Erica was looking up into his eyes, Chalice leaned down and before she knew it, his lips connected with hers. The kiss in itself seemed like magic and when it finally broke, she felt light of wind. But she opened her eyes and looked up into his anyway.

"Damn…. So I guess we on some grown man shit now huh?" Erica asked.

Chalice smiled, then raised his arm and looked at his watch.

"Hell yeah. The grown man came out about an hour ago. So what's up wit' Pumpkin?" He asked.

"She's at a friend's. Why?"

"All night?"

44

Erica nodded her head and felt butterflies in the pit of her stomach.

"So what's up? You ready to fulfill those promises you made?" He asked.

"...Uh..., which ones?" She looked seductively stupid.

"Girl quit playing. I'm trying to get into yo stuff and you holding up progress. Let's go."

Chapter Five

"I'm like the Dow Jones of rap, my stocks is high and it never was all love so stop the lies, Muthafucka's will blow yo brains out and watch you bleed. The same niggas that you trust let em watch yo seed, you gotta dead nigga cause money don't stop the greed...."
-Jadakiss Kiss of Death 1999

Chalice pushed her back onto the bed and began to kiss her from her soft lips down to her neck. He got to her nipples and took enough time to make each one as hard as the last one, then he kissed his way on down. As he came to her belly button, Erica thought he was going stop there because it had been a long time since she'd had a man eat her right. She didn't know if this young nigga knew his business or not.

Chalice pulled her thong off, damn near ripping it away. Then he raised her legs and placed them across his shoulders. He didn't really know a whole lot, but he knew that if he took his time, he would figure it out. He ran his tongue around the lips of her pussy as if they were candy. Then he decided to take a quick dip inside, only he made it a long, slow, deep dip inside and began to push his tongue in and out of her like that was his job. Erica held her breath in for so long that she almost choked. Eventually she let it out with one of those long moans that might've also been a grunt.

After about 15 minutes, the last two he spent sucking and licking her clit, she came twice back to back.

Erica grabbed his head and pulled him up. "Baby stop, come up here for a minute." She pulled him up so that they were now face to face and kissed him on the lips, tasting the traces of herself. "Damn, I hope yo young ass knows how to put this fire out," she panted.

Chalice planted one more kiss on her lips then pushed both of her legs apart and reached down to place the head of his dick at her entrance. "How about we take the time to find out?" He said as he slowly began to push up into her. The entire time he made sure to keep perfect eye contact, he didn't know if she'd ever had a man his size up in her before.

Erica almost screamed when he reached the nine inch mark.

"Oh my God.... Oh my God.... OOOh! Shit. Nigga," she chanted. She knew damn well this nigga's dick was bigger than nine and it felt like he was still pushing. Erica lifted her head and arched her back with a moan.

Chalice wasn't done yet, he felt her muscles contract and squeeze him. That was when his pelvis hit her thighs and he bounced in and out a few good times.

"Ooh...Oh... Ooh... Oh...!" She chanted, with every bounce. Erica knew that she was about to come again. Then she felt him raise her legs. "No... No... Hold up baby..., I don't think..., OH SHIT...!"

Chalice smiled as he got her all the way open and in the buck. He began to punch into her with a real purpose and for the next 20 minutes, that's what he did at an incredible speed. He had Erica coming all over herself but he didn't even begin to slow down, until he sensed the strongest nut he'd ever felt in his life.

*** *** *** *** ***

Rugar was down with the lick. But for some reason he was getting some funny vibes from this nigga Paint. He didn't really know the nigga, but when Rich had pulled him to the side and explained that the lick was on this niggas sister, Rugar had really lost all street respect for this nigga. In his eyes, didn't nothing come before your own family.

Especially greed.

"Yo, you think they sleep yet?" Rich asked.

"Yeah, come on.... Let's get it over wit," Paint replied.

Then, they all pulled out the home made stocking caps they had and began placing them over their heads. Next, they checked their guns and one by one, they started to exit the stolen car that they'd been sitting in, making their way towards the house.

*** *** *** *** ***

Chalice woke up thinking that he'd heard something but he couldn't be 100% sure. He lay in the bed, quietly listening to the night. He was thinking that if it really was something, he would hear it again. Yet for some reason, he didn't hear it again. Maybe he hadn't heard anything. He looked over to where Erica lay, curled up on her side, sleeping like a baby.

'Yeah,' he thought. *'I put my bid in on that ass tonight.'* That had been his main focus. To put it down on her so good that she'd never question him and would never give him any problems. He knew Erica was a boss and she was used to being the BOSS over others. In his eyes, there wasn't any way he was going to let her handle him the way she handled other niggas. Chalice knew there were only two real ways to get respect: You earned it or you took it. Which was what he'd done last night when he put her to sleep.

".... Wake that ass up hero! And don't do anything stupid!"

Chalice came awake at the sound of the guy's voice. At first he thought that he was dreaming. Seeing as he'd fallen asleep again. But that was until he noticed the gun pressed to his temple.

"You too Bitch! Move!" Another voice yelled.

When he looked up, Chalice saw three men, all standing

around in the room with stockings over their faces. All of them had guns. Immediately his attention was drawn to Erica, but she was sitting up in the bed all calm and collected. Erica looked into his eyes once, but then she looked directly into the barrel of the gun that was in her face.

"Bitch.... I know you got something up in here. So where it at?" One of them asked.

Chalice kept his eyes on her. He'd already figured out that they knew who Erica was and what she had. But as he watched to see what she would do, his insides tightened up as the nigga drew back and slapped her with the barrel of the gun.

"Don't make me keep asking!" He shouted and acted like he would do it again.

"A'ight," Erica said, licking her lip where the blood came from the cut. "It's in the safe. Out in the living room," she explained.

The nigga who'd slapped her, appeared to be thinking it over. "Okay, but here's the rule bitch, you give the combination and my man opens it. I don't want you getting any funny ideas, or trying to pull no gun out." He gave a somewhat crooked smile, almost as if he knew she had a gun inside. "Come on, get up!" He made her stand then turn towards the door. "Oh and just to be on the safe side, my nigga gone be in here keeping yo boyfriend company. Move bitch!"

He pushed her in the back and she stumbled forward, out of the bedroom.

Chalice was about to try and move, before the other nigga fell into step behind them. But the one standing over him must've sensed it.

"I wouldn't try nothing stupid if I were you Hero. This might not be your day."

Chalice stayed still as he sat up in the bed. He watched

49

as the second nigga went through the door behind Erica. Now it was just him and the nigga holding the gun on him. Then he remembered why he thought it was a dream.

"You know," Chalice began. "If you keep pulling hammers out on me, sooner or later you gone have to use em."

"What..., what was that nigga?" The guy with the gun asked. "I couldn't hear you. My damn finger was itching."

He didn't fully understand what Chalice had said, let alone the meaning behind it. But Chalice had put the pieces together. "Serial killers leave calling cards. You, you use the same phrase all the time," Chalice explained to him. Seeing the confusion he said, "Remember the Smiles Gas Station the other day?" The whole time Chalice had been talking, he'd been trying to throw the nigga off guard and now as he watched, he could see that he may have done just that.

Rugar was about to speak, he was stunned as he began to realize that this was the guy from the store. He wasn't paying attention as the gun moved off Chalice, just slightly. Then Rugar blinked and that was all he needed. Chalice was a street nigga for real and part of being a street nigga was learning how to fight in the streets. When his body, naked as the day that he was born, leapt into action, he immediately unleashed a series of forceful blows, not even thinking of where he was sending them. His only aim was making them connect.

Rugar was stunned. The first right hook caught him directly in the jaw and it was followed by a left jab. The two blows backed him up a few paces, but not far enough and he could do nothing. He watched as the nigga spun out from the jab and twisted his body, sending a back hand at him. He nearly went out from that one and was now starting to see that his chances were limited. Somehow Rugar finally realized that he still held the 9mm in his hand.

When the nigga drew back for another set of punches, Rugar took aim and squeezed both his eyes shut with his finger on the trigger. He didn't even care where he was shooting, just as long as this nigga stop punching him.

In the other room, just as Erica watched the nigga open the safe and begin pulling the packages of cocaine out, along with the .45 and several stacks of money that were also inside, they heard a commotion coming from the bedroom.

"What the fuck?" The one who seem to be the leader said.

They all turned slightly to look towards the bedroom door as if they expected Jesus to come walking out of the room. Then they heard the five shots being fired.

"Shit...." Paint turned away from the safe. Since Rich held the gun on Erica, who now sat in a chair, he'd been the one collecting the dope.

"Man, go see what that nigga done did," Rich told him, once again causing Paint to feel like the flunky that he was. However, before he could make the move, Rugar broke through the door.

"Man..." He was breathing hard. "Let's get out of here and fast. I know somebody heard them shots."

"Fuck...!" Paint finally spoke. "Nigga, what did you do?" He asked.

Which caused Rugar to flinch up. He twisted his face and looked at Paint sideways. "Nigga, don't raise yo fuckin voice at me. I don't even know you like that," Rugar spat.

"What?" Now Paint was getting his gangsta on.

But Rich saw where all of this was about to go. So he stepped between them. "Look...," he began. "We ain't got time for this bullshit. We gotta get out of here."

Rugar, who was sweating now, was also nodding his head. "Yeah, yeah. We gotta move," he agreed.

"Well shit, did you kill the nigga?" Paint asked. Not

even realizing that Erica had figured out who he was by now.

"I had too," Rugar stated. "The nigga tried to get wit me. So I..., Blam, blam, blam!" He motioned the action of shooting.

"Is he dead?" Rich asked.

"He should be. Shit he ain't moving," Rugar told them. "Damn nigga hits hard as fuck too." He tested his jaw.

Erica couldn't do anything but drop her head and swear that she would make Paint pay dearly for his greed.

Trai'Quan

Chapter Six

"I'm lookin for the Devil because moneys' the root of evil and kiss won't be happy until my vest'll look see through...."
-Jadakiss Kiss of Death

Six and a half keys. Rich couldn't believe it. But there it was, right there in front of him, sitting on the kitchen table. Minus the roaches and other trash, his 9mm sat next to the half key. He took a strong hit off the Kool cigarette that he was smoking and then blew out smoke rings.

"I don't see nobody. So I guess we good," Paint called out from where he stood at the window.

They were camped out in a crackhead name Lily's' apartment, at the end of Wrights Rd. and 9th Street. The apartments themselves were called Grey Stone.

"Nigga. Sit yo ass down. Ain't nobody know where we at," Rich told him. "In fact, go tell that nigga Rugar to come out here a minute."

He watched as Paint screwed his face up. He knew that for some reason, the two couldn't get along. At the moment Rugar was in the bedroom with Lily. Seeing as he turned tricks with her from time to time, he was the one that brought them there.

Paint went and knocked on the door. "Ayo Rugar, Rich said he need to see you for a minute," he called out. He then moved back over to the couch to sit down. Paint didn't even look at the dope, he'd already seen how much it was, so all he was waiting for was the split. Then he could get up out of there before he ended up killing Rugar.

Rugar stepped out of the bedroom wearing a pair of shorts, no shirt and a pair of Bugs Bunny foot flippers. He stood for a moment and looked down at Paint like he wanted to spit on him. Then he turned to Rich. "What's up

54

Hero?" He asked.

"Shit," Rich stated. "We just need to go ahead and split this shit. I know niggas got other shit they need to tend too." He glanced over to where Paint sat.

"A'ight. So what we got?" Rugar asked.

He looked down at the three separate stacks. There was two keys, two keys and two and a half keys.

"Two keys for you and two for bruh. I'm a take two and a half since we used my guns on the lick. Everybody cool wit' that?" Rich asked.

"Yeah, yeah. I'm cool," Rugar stated.

Paint, over on the couch, was mumbling to himself, but neither one of them could understand what he was saying.

"What was that P..?" Rich asked.

Paints entire body language changed. He stood and walked over to the table. "I said shit, two is more than what I thought we would come out wit a piece. Which one's mine?" He asked.

As Rich nodded, Paint picked up his two and began to turn. "Well look," he said. "It's been nice doing business wit' you niggas. But I'm about to get my hustle on. Any last words before I go?"

Both Rugar and Rich shook their heads. Then they watched as Paint threw up the deuces and left.

"Man, where the fuck did you find that lame ass nigga at?" Rugar asked.

"Pish... Been doing some hustling wit' the nigga for a while." Rich put the Kool out in the ashtray then said, "But he ain't no threat. The nigga get wrong." He nodded to the 9mm.

"Yeah, yeah. He play hero, let me know about it. I wouldn't mind clapping his ass."

And from the look on his face. Rich knew that he really wouldn't mind.

"He gone keep the half since we used his guns," Paint

said out loud to himself as he drove with the two keys sitting in the passenger seat as if they were human and listening to his every word. "Muthafucka... It was my lick! The least he could have done was give me nine ounces. Pussy ass nigga...." He continued bitching to himself, "And this lame as nigga, Rugar, the fuck he get two keys for? His bitch ass damn near fucked up the play."

He reached for the pack of Salem's on the dashboard and shook one out. Then pushed the lighter in and lit it. "These niggas think I'm something to play wit,'" he said around the cigarette butt. "But it's all good. The shit gone come back. Believe that Playa."

*** *** *** *** ***

Beep.... Beep.... Beep....

Erica stood next to the bed and looked down into Chalice's sleeping face. Except, he wasn't actually asleep. The machines were what was keeping him alive at the moment, he was in a coma.

She reached down and grasp his hand as she heard Pam, outside in the hallway, speaking with the Doctor. They'd managed to get the four slugs out of him, but the damage was already done. Chalice had also lost a lot of blood but the Doctor's said that if he made it through the night that he'd live.

She wasn't really worried about the dope, she knew that Joker would front her whatever she needed to get back on her feet, no problem. It was this nigga Pain, who she was thinking about. She was trying to decide how she was going deal with him. On the one hand, she contemplated going over to his apartment and putting a few hot ones into him. But she also knew that it wasn't a smart idea. She could always keep it on a business level and send for Smoke. Black Smoke.

In Miami the name put fear into 70% of the niggas who ran the streets at night. The other 30% didn't live in the hood and only knew the rumors, not the truths. Black Smoke was a nigga who'd spent a good part of his life in the Army. He'd been both a Ranger and in Black ops. Which meant that he was trained in ways that some minds wouldn't understand. At the age of 56, he was known to the streets of Miami as the Fog, or simply Smoke, because of the way he moved.

He no longer worked for the government and Erica wasn't sure why. Something had happened and the way she got it, the government turned their backs on him. Now Smoke worked for Joker. Whenever Joker had a problem that he decided needed some extra muscle, he sent in Smoke. The only problem was, usually once Smoke came and left, the body count would be higher than it was before.

So she was thinking she could use Smoke, knowing that Joker would send him if she asked. But she still had to find out who the other two niggas were first.

*** *** *** *** ***

"We ain't, going nowhere.... We ain't going nowhere, we can't be stopped.... Bad Boys for life." Rich bobbed his head to the music, bouncing as he whipped the Yukon through traffic. Fresh out of the switch shop, he'd given Danny Boy ten ounces for the truck, fully loaded, paint job, music and all.

The Switch Shop was a chop shop ran by this white guy, named Danny Boy. All of the dope boys fucked with him because the switch over was so good that you couldn't tell, unless you knew to look for the serial numbers on the motor.

Rich swerved into Barton village like he owned the place. This being the first time he'd ever been able to flex like this, he damn sure wanted everybody to see him. He had to go back down to OS, Ole Savannah Rd was where he had decided to put down at. Between South Side Apartments and Turpin Hill, or rather Kent Circle. He knew that he'd be able to really put it down like he wanted to and if he did it just right, he would be able to double his two keys into four keys with no time. Yeah, he thought, that was the plan.

*** *** *** *** ***

Paint decided to keep it local, since he already had roots in Williamsburg and the trailer park on Deans Bridge Rd. He was going to keep moving his shit in the same area, only now he could really get his grind on. Paint already knew that his main problem would be keeping his nose clean. He was a Miami nigga at heart and the majority of hustlers from Miami put a little coke up their noses from time to time. But his thing was that he liked to do it a little more than most. Nevertheless, he told himself that this time he was going monitor the shit and not get out of hand with it.

He knew most people often wondered why he could never get on his feet, especially with his sister being major in the game. In truth, it never was her fault. Erica had tried to put him on when she first got the dope, but his nose kept him down and he'd learned to blame everybody except himself, for his short comings.

Now things were different. Now he had a real chance. Before, the most dope he ever touched all at once was 18 ounces and even then it hadn't all been his. He still had to answer to Erica.

"Dumb ass bitch," he grumbled. "Now who got the power?"

What he wasn't thinking about, was that Erica still had connections and he didn't. In the dope game you could be dead broke, cops done hit you and either took everything, or you had to flush it, but if you had just one solid connection, you never really lost anything in the first place. You only had a setback.

*** *** *** *** ***

"I could help you sell it."

Rugar looked up from where he just took the cookie out of the pot and put it on the table. Lily sat across from him. Having helped cut up the first cookie.

"I ain't trying to be funny baby, but I'd have to be crazy to put crack in a smokers hand and expect to come out on top." He watched as she sucked her teeth.

"I'm just saying. You ain't got to give me the dope, I could bring the business to you. I know everybody who smoke, the one's who got the money and the ones who can make money," she explained.

The more he thought about it, the more sense it made. Rugar wasn't no dope dealer, he was a Jackboy, always had been. But he knew a little something about the trade and he knew enough to know that he wasn't about to be standing out on no corner playing with the cops. "A'ight. You got a point," he told her. "I'll just keep yo bills paid and let you smoke real good. We cool on that?"

"Hell yeah!" Lily nodded. If there was one thing she knew, it was that Rugar was drunk over her stuff. Lily knew she had some good pussy. Shit she had learned how to fuck when she was 12 years old. Having been repeatedly raped by an older nigga in the neighborhood, she'd been too scared and too stupid to tell. But by the time she turned 15, she'd pretty much mastered the art of sex. Now everybody knew that she had that good-good.

She smiled as Rugar set about cutting up the cookie. She had some long term plans for his ass. She was going to do a whole lot of smoking for free.

Extended Clip

Paris had been standing next to his Navigator, talking to Pumpkin, when Erica pulled into the driveway. They both knew what had happened so they knew where she'd just come from.

"How you doing Paris?" Erica asked once she got out of the Range.

"I'm good. What about you? Is Chalice okay?" He asked. Paris didn't really know Chalice like that. Mostly because they moved in different circles and Chalice was a little older.

"He'll make it, but he's still in a coma." Erica watched as they both dropped their heads at the news. Then she excused herself and went into the house.

"I don't know what nigga made that move," Paris told Pumpkin. "But when my old man finds out who it was, there's gone be some problems."

Pumpkin looked at him as he spoke and she thought that she could sense something else in his words. Kind of an underlying meaning or something. "You said that like you gone ride too," she stated straight out.

"I might," Paris told her. "You know y'all is like family to us. Besides, Erica about to be my mother-in-law."

"Oh really?" She twisted her face up. "Ain't nobody said nothing about no marriage. So where you get that from?"

"Girl stop playing." He laughed, then he pushed off the side of his truck and began to walk towards the driver's door. "Listen. I've got some shit to do, but you gone call me later right?"

"Mmm hmm, I'll see what I can do," she said.

"Girl, stop playing."

In the house, Erica was standing in the bathroom in shock. She couldn't believe it and she was holding the test right there in her hands. But she still couldn't believe it. Pregnant.... After one night?

"Damn that young nigga don't play," she muttered but she shook her head, still finding it hard to believe.

Chapter Seven

"My niggas on the left, rag shit to death, my hoods on the right, wild for tonight, my clan in the front, let your feet stop, killer bee's in the back come on an attack....."
-Wutang clan 36 chambers

11 ½ Months Later.....

Her 17th birthday party wasn't actually a party. Pumpkin had a few of her friends over and they spent most of their time playing with her baby brother, Giavoni, who somehow seem to realize that he was getting a whole lot of female attention at two months old.

Erica and Pam had gone to the hospital. Chalice had come out of his coma that morning, so she knew her mom would be spending a good deal of time there. Which was why she agreed to keep baby G, so that Erica could have some time alone with Chalice. Pumpkin was wondering what he was going to say when he found out he had a son. A whole lot had changed since he'd been shot and she felt sorry for her Uncle. At first there hadn't been any news about the robbery in the streets, but a little more than six months ago, the rumor got out. Word was, Paint was the one behind the lick and since he was doing real good for himself, it all made sense.

It had surprised her to find out that Erica already knew and since she'd been pregnant she'd used the time to find out who the other two niggas had been. Now, it all boiled down to what Chalice might want to do about it.

"Hold up, hold up.... Why y'all keep acting like a nigga fragile or something?" Chalice asked.

They had both hugged him like he was on the verge of breaking or something.

"Nah nigga, don't nobody wanna hurt yo sensitive ass," Pam laughed.

Chalice had taken four slugs. Two in the stomach, one in the chest and one to the temple. The bandages were still on his head and the doctors said there might be some trouble with headaches for a while.

"Sensitive," Chalice responded. "Yeah, a nigga took four shots and still breathing. You call that sensitive?"

"Nigga chill out. You betta be thankful yo ass still breathing. I almost thought my grandbaby was gone grow up without a father," Pam stated.

Which made Chalice pay close attention to what was going on. Erica hadn't spoken yet, she sat quietly on the side of the bed.

"Grandbaby..., uh...., unless you've adopted a baby since I've been asleep, you talking sideways on me," he wavered.

"Nah.... You and Erica made this one," Pam smiled. "We even had a blood test done right before you woke up. So yeah, it's yours."

Chalice looked from her to Erica. He watched as she nodded. "Damn.... And we only did it once," he replied as a big grin spread across his face.

"Which means we gone have to suite that guy up next time," Erica warned.

"Damn, so what we got. Boy or girl?"

"A boy. His name's Giavoni. He's at home with Pumpkin and her friends," she explained.

"Giavoni... Ain't that Italian or something?" He asked. "What, you gone make him a mob boss one day?"

"That's up to you. But we'll talk about all of that when you come home. Oh, you'll be living with me, Pumpkin and the baby. It's kind of crowded over at Pam's new house," she told him.

"New house…, crowded?" Chalice turned and looked at Pam. "Don't tell me you dropped a load too while I been asleep."

"No..., but me and Cujo did get a house out in Woodlake

and Paris is still there for a minute," she told him and then paused. "But here's the thing, we're about to get married. So that would make Paris your..., uh..., step brother," she said and laughed.

For a minute he sat there looking stupid. A son and a step-brother. He was happy for his mother.

Sometime later, when Pam left and it was just him and Erica, the conversation changed.

"So what's up? You know who did it?" He asked.

"Uhg. Yeah. But you ain't exactly in no condition to be talking about seeing nobody," she told him.

"That ain't the point. I just wanna know who that nigga was who hit me up. I've got some plans for that ass," He explained.

"Well, that would be Rugar," Erica told him. "He's a low budget Jackboy from Washington DC. But he ain't the real problem."

This caught his attention. He saw that there seem to be more on her mind. "Oh yeah? So what exactly is the problem?"

"Hold up. Let me lay this out for you first. Then you make your mind up," she told him.

"Since Cujo had two and a half keys at the time they pulled the robbery. He was able to stay afloat. But I still had to call in a favor with my people down 95...," she said and then paused a moment. "Joker came through and blessed me wit' four more keys. But that was then, I've paid that back. So now I'm holding something like 12 kilos, of which Cujo and his crew are moving right now. My next re-up is in a month."

Chalice thought about all of that. Business was good for her, he could see that. Yet, he still didn't see what that had to do with him killing these niggas. "A'ight.... So you bounced back... That's all love. But I'm tryin to dead these niggas and all I need is a ratchet and some information," he told her.

"Here's the thing." Erica became more serious. "I'm going to put you on. When I go get the 12 keys next month, I want to introduce you to Joker. In doing that, the move is this, I'm going to give you control of the 12 keys and let you run that part of the business, while I run the club and raise Giavoni." She took a moment to let that sink in. Seeing that he was thinking it over, she felt better.

"So what you're saying is I'm a made nigga now," Chalice stated.

"In a sense. But you've still got a lot of work to do and in the process of all that. You'll have to move differently," she explained.

"So wait a minute. You telling me that I'm not gone be able to kill them niggas? Girl stop playing, cause them niggas gone die," he said with passion.

Inside, Erica was smiling. It seemed like the shooting itself had unleashed something no one knew was inside of him.

Chalice, on his end, was thinking about the 12 keys. He honestly didn't know the street value of it. But between him, Que and John-John, he knew that they would figure it out. He was also thinking about Paris. Maybe he could pull him in. "Okay, so smart niggas move smart. Now tell me who did what."

"Paint and his partner Rich. They the ones who did it," she told him. "At the moment it seems like their doing pretty good. The six and a half keys they got, put them in. I think they've doubled it at least twice since then, but they're doing real good."

That was all Chalice needed to hear. The DC nigga, Rugar, was the one who shot him, but it would be all three of them would pay the price.

*** *** *** *** ***

Rich sat in his new four bedroom house, in the large custom detailed den, holding a glass of Alize in one hand and a blunt in the other. *'Yeah,'* he thought to himself. *'Sugar Hill was heaven on the top for black folks.'* To him, this was what life was meant to be. A lot of money, no kids and a bad ass bitch to make him look good. Plus the bitch was white.

Tina was only 5'4 and 129lbs, a natural red head with a body like a sista. She had the ass of a dream. Nice and plump, not that slanted tear drop shit.

"Yeah, this shit is sweet," he said out loud, speaking to no one but himself. Then his mind went to thoughts of business. It sure felt good this past year, with him being that nigga for a change. Rugar was doing good, he and Lily, but that nigga Paint looked like he was about to fall off. Word in the streets was, Paint had been snorting cocaine for a while and then he started smoking funny joints. Just three days ago, Rich heard that he was turning tricks with crack head named Wanda. He knew if that was true, then it wouldn't be long before he was on the pipe.

Rich wasn't really all that surprised. He'd seen that the nigga was weak. Pushing those thoughts aside he remembered that he had to take his mom and little sister, Renee some money. Renee was only three years younger than him, making her 27. But she had two kids by a nothing ass nigga named Killa Black. Who the nigga killed, Rich didn't know, but the nigga wasn't shit and he wasn't doing shit for those kids. Even though Rich was all about himself, he still cared about his family. That was the one thing he would take a nigga to war about, with no understanding needed.

*** *** *** *** ***

Since Paris had started moving some dope, he'd been spending a lot of time in Trending Manor. That was his trap spot and also where he and Pumpkin were standing in the parking lot when Troop pulled in and parked next to her BMW x3, which Erica had given her for a birthday gift.

"Look here Pumpkin, where yo girl at?" Troop called out.

At first Paris was tempted to confront the nigga for his lack of respect. But he didn't.

"Who Shae? Nigga didn't you get the news, she's got a nigga," Pumpkin informed him.

This caused Troop to laugh. "Who, that nigga B' Nice? Man that nigga can't even carry my shoes, much less hold on to a bad bitch like Shae." He laughed again.

"You know what?" Paris spoke up, giving him the evil eye look. "You a real disrespectful ass nigga." He'd been trying as hard as he could to overlook the nigga, but now he was just fed the fuck up.

"Oh.... My bad baby boy," Troop said. "I wouldn't want to offend the infamous Paris himself. Pisssh. Yeah right."

Since he'd been leaning against the side of his Navigator with his arms crossed, Paris pushed himself off and moved over to where Troop sat inside of his Durango Truck. He stopped and looked the nigga straight in his eyes.

"Look nigga, you don't really want it wit' P...," Paris stated. "So don't start some shit you ain't built to deal wit.' Because you and I both know that I will fuck you up. So the best thing for you to do, might be to pull on off." Then Paris stood back and watched as the nigga tried to act as if he wanted to say something. Instead, he smile and backed his truck out while throwing up the deuces.

Paris was still watching him drive away and wasn't aware of Pumpkin walking up behind him.

"Baby, don't let that nigga upset you," she said.

"Yeah, I know right. That nigga ain't even worth the air

he breaths."

"I know, but he gone get his sooner than he thinks," she told him.

Causing him to look over at her. "Oh yeah. By who?"

"You know that nigga works for Rugar. That's the nigga who shot Chalice. Shiiiit.... Him, Paint and Rich gone get it when Chalice gets right," she explained to him.

Paris didn't even question her on that. He'd also heard the rumors in the streets that those were the three who robbed Erica and put Chalice in a coma. Common sense told him that Pumpkin only spoke the truth.

Erica was deep in her own thoughts as she drove the Audi QS. She'd been thinking about Chalice and the fact that he was either gone be passive or too aggressive once he came home. She suspected, even a nigga who'd been good all of his life, would change after being shot. She'd heard stories of weak niggas turning into Superman niggas and hard niggas turning into bitches. But it was hard to say about Chalice. No one could say that he was either hard or soft because he hadn't been in the streets. So anything was possible.

Chalice couldn't believe he was sitting up in a hospital room watching old re-runs of Sanford and Son. He really wasn't watching the TV, his mind was off somewhere else. There were flashbacks of the robbery at the store, then the nigga being jacked in the streets and eventually he saw himself being shot in Erica's bedroom. Even though he didn't notice it, his body jumped each time he saw Rugar squeeze off a round.

He'd tried to live right, he did. But society was fucked up and their concepts were fucking with him. The cops were never where they were needed, Whites didn't care about Blacks and niggas loved them more then they loved their own. Twice now he'd been somebody else's victim. Twice. But never again. The very next time, he would be the beast.

Chapter Eight

"In a mob meeting, keep quiet when the God speaking, squeeze my joint until my muthafuckin palms squeaking...."
-Jadakiss Kiss of Death

Chalice really didn't feel like he needed a wheel chair, but they made him ride in one all the way downstairs. It was the only way they were letting him leave, five months after he'd awakened. It took him that long to get use to his body again and in that time, he'd exercised and read several books. Message to the Blackman in America, which was his favorite.

As the elevator stopped the nurse pushed him out. He knew that Erica was picking him up. Chalice thought about how the character in the book had a split personality and how he came up in the hustle. There was a lot to learn from it, which was why he held on to the book and intended to read them again.

The nurse pushed him to the double doors, which slid open and the bright light of the day hit his eyes. It took him a moment to adjust, but once his vision came into focus, he saw Erica standing in front of a truck. First he saw her and the Apple bottom, denim wash jeans she wore. She was showing the extra weight she'd gained in her hips.

"What's up baby, you like?" She asked.

Chalice stood up out of the chair and gave her another up and down look. "Yeah, but we gotta do something about them ab's. Drop about three inches," he said.

"Nigga..., I was talkin about your truck," she stated.

His attention went straight to the cocaine white, Cadillac Escalade ESV, all-wheel drive, sitting on the Ashanti rims. "Oh yeah?" He looked at her as she held the keys out to him. "Mine huh?"

Chalice leaned forward and kissed her on the cheek. He opened the passenger side door for her then patted her on the ass as she turned to get in. He then slid in himself, behind the wheel.

*** *** *** *** ***

"Ayo nigga, you heard?" Troop damn near shouted the words into his cellphone, sounding all hyperactive.

"Nah, nah Junior. What's up?" Rugar asked. Talking like he'd just left DC yesterday. In the hoods up there, everyone was a 'junior.' Kind of like in Atlanta where everyone was a 'Shawty' and Chicago everyone was a 'Joe'. In New York everyone was a 'Son'.

"That nigga coming home today," Troop stated.

But Rugar was slightly confused. He didn't know what in the hell Troop was talking about. "Listen Hero, what nigga you talkin bout? There's a lot of niggas out here," he said.

"Nah bruh. That nigga Chalice," Troop put the name to the information. "Man I got it from this lil bitch that be around Paris' girl. Somebody went to pick the nigga up."

Rugar sat up straight on the sofa. Everyone knew by now what had gone down. That stupid ass nigga Paint had bragged about it to half of Augusta. The same way they knew this nigga Chalice hadn't died that day, he'd been in a coma.

"A'ight Junior. I'm a get back to you. Preciate the news," Rugar said and ended the call.

He dialed Rich's number. Common sense said if niggas in the streets knew what the business was, then this nigga had to know.

Ten minutes later, Rich ended the call, then looked at Jue-Jue. He'd been in the process of dropping off a package to his two lieutenants, Jue-Jue and Baby Chris, when

Rugar's call had come through.

"Alright, what was I saying?" He asked.

"Oh.... Some shit about you fixing to go see some people about a package," Jue-Jue reminded him.

"Oh, yeah," Rich caught up. The conversation with Rugar wasn't even a factor in his eyes. At the moment he was thinking about his next pick up. In the time since they'd robbed Erica, he'd really put his foot in it. Having taken a good long vacation in Miami some months ago, he'd met a nigga they called 'Big Afrika.' A well-known drug King pin with ties to some cartel. No one knew which one, but Big Afrika had an unlimited supply of dope.

At the moment, Rich was doing heavy business with Big Afrika. Hearing about Erica and her boyfriend was the last thing on his mind. The way he saw it, he'd deal with that problem when it became a problem.

*** *** *** *** ***

"Yo, I'm telling you," Que was in the process of explaining. "I've got all types of Hammers and Ratchets on deck. All you got to do is put up the loot and I can get whatever."

At the moment Chalice stood there thinking the three of them, him, Que and John-John, were all standing out at the green box in front of Erica's house, in Pepperidge. He'd already explained to them what he wanted to do, but for some reason there seemed to be some kinks in the plan.

Mostly when he thought about how Erica had explained, that over time, Rich, Paint and Rugar had all gotten their weight up. They wouldn't be easy to get at and here it was, just three of them.

Amazingly, that was his main thought when Paris' Navigator pulled up behind Que's Explorer and Paris got out along with another young nigga. Chalice watched as they both walked over to where they stood.

"What up P?" Chalice gave Paris a pound then looked at the other nigga. "Sup duke?"

"Sup..."

Paris peeped the vibe so he stepped in. "Aye Chalice, this my nigga B' Nice. He be rocking with Pumpkins' friend Shae."

Chalice nodded. He'd met Shae and didn't have any problem with her. "A'ight. Yo, both of them in the house with Erica and the baby," he told them. "Y'all can go on in if you want."

But Paris gave him a different look and then he smiled at them. "Nah big Bruh. We came to see you," he said, leaving Chalice vexed.

"Oh yeah? So what you got going on?" Chalice watched as Paris looked at all three of them.

"Sup' Que, John-John?" He spoke. Then he turned his attention back to Chalice. "Figured you was about to make a move and me and Nice wanted in. The way I see it," Paris told them. "It's just three of y'all against about 10 or 15 of them. Right?"

"Yeah, that's about the size of it," Chalice told him.

"Shit. Add me and Nice to the deck and it should be about even," Paris suggested.

Chalice actually thought about it. He even liked the idea. There was just one problem. "Damn bruh, I like yo numbers. But what Cujo gone say when he finds out?" Chalice asked then watched as Paris smiled.

"Big Bruh, who you think sent us over here? B' Nice was one of Pops top dudes. Now Pops is letting Redd step up. He sent me and B' Nice to join your team, but it's all on you Bruh...."

Chalice gave it some thought. Then he looked back at Que. "Can you get enough guns for a five man team?"

"God..., you ain't listening to me," Que told him in

frustration. "You get the loot. When we go meet this snowman, he gone have whatever we need. All you got to do is get the loot and let me set it up."

After he explained. Chalice looked back at Paris and B' Nice. "There's gone be a lot of blood in the streets before this is all over. But here's the thing, this team I'm building," he paused to look at each man. "It's not just to go after them niggas," Chalice continued. "You four niggas will be like the Four Horsemen in the Bible, the four niggas who bring death and change to a world that needs it. So this isn't just about killing, it's also about moving all of this dope I'm about to touch. So all of you niggas wanna get money?" He asked.

"Fuckin right!" John-John said.

"No doubt God!" Que added.

"We wit' you," B' Nice said.

"Just say the word Big Bruh," Paris told him.

Chalice nodded. "Then it's official. From this point on, y'all niggas are the Four Horsemen. Que, make that call, I'm a go in here and get this money." With that said, Chalice started towards the house at the same time Que pulled out his cellphone.

*** *** *** *** ***

TWO HOURS LATER.

The meeting took place under the Walton Way over Pass, down near the 401 jail and directly behind the Food stamp office. All five of them stood there with the white guy named Gary and looked at the guns in the back of his Hummer. There were all types of guns, from handguns to assault rifles.

"This is an Ambush 5.56. It's a US version of the AR-15 semi-automatic. Good guns will run you about $1800. I've got two for I'll sell you for three grand," Gary explained. "Then I've got this Black rain, another AR-15, this one is a .308 platform. It's highly effective and shoots 7.62 Nato rounds. It weighs 9lbs, 4 Oz's, with an 18 inch stainless, double straight fluted barrel and 20 round Pmag. I've got one of those and it's about two grand flat. I can let it go for $1500."

Chalice watched and listened as he went on to explain a number of rifles and handguns. Then he pulled out six bullet proof vests and some sound suppressors. In the end. They got both the Ambush 5.56's and the Black rain, along with two Mossberg pump 4.9 mm Taurus editions, the silencers and all six vests. All of which came with ammunition.

"That's a pretty big order," Gary replied.

He watched as Que, John-John, Paris and B' Nice pulled out the guns they'd chosen. But Chalice was still looking. At least he was until his eyes kept coming back to four certain guns.

"Let me get all four of them too," he said nodding to the twin .44 chrome plated, Desert Eagle, long barrel pistols and the two 9mm Chrome plated, Desert Eagle short barrels.

"You sure you want the two short barrels? I've got a couple longs at the house," Gary told him.

"Nah, those are for my wife," Chalice told him as he picked the guns up. "Call em a late birthday present."

Once all of the guns were put into their trucks, Chalice gave Gary a gym bag with the money inside of it. "You should have five to ten grand extra in there. Hit my man up when you get some more ammo," he said.

Gary nodded and took the bag.

*** *** *** *** ***

"What's up? You hear anything?" Rugar asked.

But both Tommy Bird and Roe Dogg shook their heads.

"Man niggas ain't saying shit," Tommy Bird said.

Rugar had told all of his boys to keep their ears to the streets. He wanted to be up on anything that happen lately.

"And ain't nobody seen this nigga," Roe Dogg added.

Rugar nodded. Still deep in his own thoughts. He wasn't exactly sure how to go about dealing with the issue. Rich acted like it wasn't a threat to him, but then too, Rich wasn't in the room with the nigga that night. He tested his jaw again. 16 months later and he could still feel the punches the nigga hit him with then. On top of that, he'd been the one who shot the nigga. Rugar knew niggas wouldn't forget who shot them. "Well, y'all niggas stay on point," he instructed both of them.

Mentally he was telling himself that this shit wasn't over. If this young nigga had any buck in him, it was about to be hot outside and somebody was going to feel it.

Trai'Quan

Chapter Nine

"Sex....ual healing baby, it feels good to me...."
-Marvin Gaye

The music from the Escalade wasn't too loud, nor was it real low, but everyone could hear Marvin as he sung the words to whatever woman held his attention at that time. Might have been Tammy Terrell, but it was the music itself that made Erica walk over to look out the window where she watched as Chalice's cocaine white Escalade pulled up next to her QS.

The music stopped after a while and then she watched as Chalice got out and Giavoni followed him. Both of them were dressed like a set of street thugs, like twins. They wore denim jeans and cream-colored Sean John shirts, with Timberland Euro boots that were trimmed in a cream color and had gummy soles. She didn't even pay any attention to the diamond studded, closed Rolex that he wore.

It had been their father and son day, which meant that she had no idea where he had taken her baby, or what they had been doing. By the time they entered the house, she met them at the door and greeted Giavoni, who was laughing and smiling at her.

"Looks like y'all had fun. He ain't high is he?"

Chalice kissed her and stepped around her. "Nah, lil dude ain't wanna hit the blunt," he laughed. "So what you been up to?"

"Not a whole lot. I talked to Joker," she told him. Chalice knew all about Joker, she'd already given him the rundown so that business would go the way she'd planned.

"Oh yeah. So everything good?"

"Yeah we good. It's gone be next weekend. Will your team be alright until we get back?"

She'd given him three and a half kilos to work with until

this deal went down and he'd used it to get his four horsemen established. He had told them not to move big yet. To hustle just enough so that their faces were known in the streets and once he hit them with the next package, then they could pretty much do whatever they wanted to. "They gone be alright. But where Pumpkin at? I don't see her BMW."

"Knowing her, she's probably somewhere with Paris. Or chilling with Shae," she explained.

Chalice took a seat and chilled in the front room. It wasn't long before he began to reflect back on his conversation with B' Nice, the day he'd taken him to get a ride.

"So what type of hustles are you into?" Chalice asked. He could see that B' Nice felt put on the spot, but everyone else out there he already knew.

"Not much. I use to boost cars, did a little of this and a little of that. Why you ask?" B' Nice asked.

Chalice had become silent and all eyes had gone to him. B' Nice had wondered why so much focus was on it until Chalice spoke. That's when he began to understand.

"Well actually, it's like this, since I can tell that Shae is a good girl and she's Pumpkins best friend, you could say I just wanted to see what type of nigga she was drawn to." He paused a moment. "In case you didn't know because of my age, I sort of take this step-daughter thing to heart and I know Paris, her bringing you into the folds means one thing, but I still had to get a feel for you, for myself." He stopped and waited a moment. "The reason I asked about your hustle is because I don't need any stupid niggas on this team. I need niggas who can think and in times of need, out think the cops."

B' Nice had taken some time to think about that. "Okay, so what exactly are you saying?" B' Nice asked.

"Good question. Well, it's like this, what I'm building is

a family and everybody in it is responsible for every other person. In the streets some niggas find group support to be too hard for them." Chalice paused in thought a moment. *"There are two things I hate, the first is a rat. I can't stand niggas who eat cheese. The second, is a lack of support. That shit is New Jack City where Nino was stressing he was his brother's keeper, but in the end, he fucked up more than anybody else."* Chalice watched as everybody nodded to the thought. *"You niggas remember that, this ain't a movie. This shit is real! On that Biggie song where it says,* 'We lie together, we cried together. I swear to God I hope we fuckin cried together. I swear to God I hope we fuckin die together....' *That's the Four Horsemen baby! That's what this all means. So, Believe in that!"*

Coming back to himself, Chalice realized all the work he was about to put into the plan he was fixing to set into motion.

"What was that?" He asked as he shook his head. Erica was talking to him and he hadn't heard her.

"Did you take care of your business?" She asked again.

"Yeah. It's gone take some work, but I believe we can put it down in a couple months." He was talking about the old club he'd just leased. The plan was to remodel it and name it the Black Chalice. A new strip club, down on Broad Street.

Sitting next to them, Giavoni yawned. He was sleepy. "Let me go put this nigga down," she said.

When she left, Chalice reached over, picked up the phone and dialed a number.

"Hello." A female answered.

"Kandy. Where that nigga Que at?"

"Oh, he right here. How you doing Chalice?" She asked.

"I'm alright. Just a few headaches. But nothing too serious."

Kandy had been one of the nurses at the hospital. She

still worked there but was seeing Que now. They'd met one day when Que came to see Chalice.

There was a little noise on the other end of the phone, then he heard Que ask, "Peace God. How you feel?"

"Aye Peace Allah, I'm still breathing. Just called to see how business been," Chalice told him. "Yo you paged me?"

"Yeah, yeah. That was earlier, but the P came through. He picked them ends up, it's all good. But yo..., what you think about Sandbar Ferry Rd?" Que asked.

Erica had put Giavoni to bed and came back into the room but she didn't say anything.

"That's that nigga, Paint's area, ain't it?" He asked.

"Yeah, but word on the streets is that the nigga ain't handling business. They say that the nigga smoking his business up," Que explained.

Chalice already knew this, but he wasn't sure that Erica knew it. He did catch her eye as she sat on the end of the sofa. "Go ahead and have somebody check it out. But don't make no plans until we get this re-up. We gone see what happens next week," he explained.

*** *** *** *** ***

He hit the pipe hard, almost used his last breath doing it. Both of his lungs filled up with the smoke from the piece of crack that was in the pipe. Paint still couldn't believe he felt as good as he did.

"A'ight, a'ight..., c... c... come on m... man. It... It's my turn... p... p...pass that... shit...," Bruce stuttered.

When his ability to think straight returned to him, Paint looked over at the other nigga like he was crazy. *'How this nigga gone tell me to hurry up on my dope,'* he thought. But even as he had the thought, he still passed the pipe and then sat back while Bruce got his smoke on. He didn't necessarily pass it because he was scared of Bruce. Nah,

81

Bruce was his man. He passed it because it wasn't but a hit left in it anyway. Even though Bruce was his man, he still felt like Bruce needed to bring more to the party besides his lips. Either way it didn't matter because he was about to get off the dope anyway. He'd already checked out one of the centers down on Telfair Street. He just wanted to smoke up the last of this package and get it all out of his system before he got clean.

His eyes locked in on Bruce. The dope was gone but the nigga still acted like some more was about to magically come out of the pipe. Paint shook his head.

*** *** *** *** ***

"B' you need to start seeing reality nigga. You out here getting money and shit, I would think you knew better then to listen to gossip," Tommy Bird was in the process of saying. "Ain't no such thing as Four Horsemen. Nigga, you ain't got to try and impress us."

"Yeah, you still cool wit' us. Big dreams and all," Roe Dogg laughed.

But B' Nice looked from one of them to the other. He thought these niggas were crazy as he shook his head.

Rugar's boys had been out hustling for a while now. The only reason B' Nice was ever in their hood hustling was because Shae also lived in Harrisburg.

"Man, y'all niggas is pathetic. What, you don't think shit like that is possible?" B' Nice asked.

Part of what Chalice told them to do was put the name in the streets. Tell as many people about the Four Horsemen as possible. But not to tell nobody who they really were.

"I know one thing," B' Nice continued. "Y'all niggas better hope y'all ain't around when the slugs start flying. Word is, once the smoke clears, there ain't gone be but four niggas standing."

"Yeah right," Tommy Bird laughed. "And you think Rugar sitting back scared of a rumor. Man, who them niggas done killed? Nobody."

"Who they work for? That nigga you fuckin wit' these days?" Roe Dogg asked.

Word was, Chalice was building a team. But nobody knew who was on it, they only assumed that since B' Nice talked to Shae, and Paris went with Pumpkin, that meant Paris and B' Nice were around one another a lot. Niggas thought that Paris would have something to do with it.

"Whatever man. Just don't sleep and don't say a nigga ain't gave y'all no heads up," B' Nice was in the process of saying when Shae pulled up in his Yukon Denali. B' Nice gave them one last look then shook his head as he walked over and got into the truck.

"Ay, B' Nice. Tell them niggas we shakin in our boots!" Roe Dogg called out.

But B' Nice didn't even acknowledge it. Shae put the truck in drive and pulled off.

As she drove with Biggie Smalls bumping in the CD player, B' Nice thought about his life. He was a nigga who never had nothing. He grew up in the projects, on welfare, with two sisters and a brother. His moms always found a way to get by. As he got older, he'd stolen a few cars and did a few short Juvenile bids. Then Cujo popped up and gave him a shot at the streets. He made the best out of it and soon, they weren't as poor as they had been. Then somehow, he ended up with Shae.

He'd made some money with Cujo, but not like what he had going on with Chalice. The first thing Chalice did, other than buying the guns, was made sure they all had rides. Que's busted up Explorer was now a Ford Expedition. John-John pushed a Suburban extended cab and B' Nice now had the Denali.

"Can you believe this nigga?" Tommy Bird asked.

Both he and Roe Dogg were still standing out hustling, as B' Nice left with Shae.

"Yeah, I know," Roe Dogg scoffed. "Fucking Four Horsemen. Nigga been reading too much of the Bible and shit."

"Yeah and them nigga's Jue-Jue and Baby Chris was talkin bout it the other day," Tommy Bird put in.

This however, caught Roe Dogg's attention. "Yeah," he said.

"Some bitches been spreading the shit throughout South Side. Shit, I thought you already heard about it," Tommy Bird said.

They both fell silent. Both in their own thoughts about the issue.

Trai'Quan

Chapter Ten

Miami Florida

The sign some ways back said, *'Welcome to Dade County'*, but Chalice wasn't really paying any attention as he drove the rented Mercedes Benz Sedan. Both Erica and Pumpkin were in the back seat and both had dozed off while Paris sat in the passenger seat next to Chalice.

At first, the trip would have been made by just him and Erica, but apparently this Joker guy knew Pumpkin since she'd been a baby and he suggested that Erica bring her. Plus, Chalice had never been to Miami and Paris knew the city. So it was ideal for them to all hang out together. Especially with Paris becoming his first in charge. The trip was giving them the time they needed to bond.

"They say I walk around like I got an '8' on my chest. Nah, that's a semi auto and a vest on my chest....."

The boot leg, 50 Cent, *'Get Rich or die Trying'* that Que bought when he'd went back to New York was bumping in the CD player.

Chalice couldn't help but smile. Because of the move his lawyer had pulled. His whole plan had been to crush Paint, Rich and Rugar financially, before he got them physically. Using Erica's dope, they now had a successful business. Rugar had three pool halls and a bar that were doing good. Rich had a car lot and Paint owned a limo service. What made him smile was the two part lick he'd put down right before they left on this trip. He was wondering how Paint was dealing with the reality.

"I wish Rugar had fuckin killed that nigga!" Paint stated

out loud. He was pissed and he doubted that words could express the way he truly felt. Since he'd finished crushing up the rock he was about to smoke, he leaned forward and picked up the glass pipe off the kitchen table. Next he put a small piece of the crack in it, then picked up his lighter.

Paint inhaled deep as he listened to the crackling sounds of the dope burning. He brought the pipe down and sat it on the table. His lungs were still filled with the smoke as he leaned back in the chair. His head fell back and he looked up at the light, then he exhaled the smoke. The high was something he just couldn't explain. Way more than a weed high. Fuckin unbelievable.

"Now let me think about this shit," he said to no one other than himself. He didn't know where Bruce was.

Just last week he'd found out that he lost the Limo service because the bank that was holding his note suddenly pushed for their money. The money that he couldn't pay. So they claimed to have foreclosed on the lease by force. Then a day later, he'd been informed that the bank sold the company and to who of all people? Erica. From what he heard, it was really that nigga Chalice, he'd just put it in her name. Lately the nigga had become a problem and now that problem seem to be growing bigger.

On top of all that, just two days ago that nigga Chalice and his so called Four Horsemen, ran up in East Boundry and had a shootout with his boys. Paint had people from the barbershop right behind smiles all the way down to the end of the street. They'd killed several of his boys on Walker Street, a few in River Glenn and some in Oak Village. When the ones who didn't get shot saw what went down, they up and ran away.

"Pussy niggas fuckin ran…, from five niggas!" He still didn't understand that. Paint exploded in rage and with a sweep of his arm he knocked everything off the table. Then he jumped up and took the table with him. "Pussy ass niggas! The fuck y'all gone let some niggas take my shit?" He screamed. Then he began to tear the kitchen apart. After a while Paint found himself on his knees inside the living room and lying on the floor in front of him was the .357 magnum. But his thoughts weren't of suicide, he'd been thinking about murder and he had two faces in his mind's eye.

"But what if I miss?" He asked. It may have seemed strange, but he'd been talking to the gun as if it had a voice of its own. Either way, his mind was made up. So what if he didn't succeed, it would still be a strike against the two causing him this pain.

"Dear God...," Paint bowed his head and began to pray.

*** *** *** *** ***

The police couldn't understand it. The snitches, or informers, whatever they wanted to call themselves, all spoke about the same thing, Four Horsemen.

"What the fuck did they do, ride four horses down East Boundry like cowboys and gun everybody down? How the fuck did they gallop in and gallop out without a single Police Officer seeing them?" The Chief of Police said to the room of officers before him. "East Boundry is only a few streets over. It's practically our fuckin back yard and yet, no one saw anything? No one knows anything? Give me a fuckin break here."

As he looked at each of his detectives and the officers who patrolled that area, he could see that they felt a shame about it.

"We've got what, eight, nine bodies in the morgue? And God only knows how many aggravated assaults. Somebody had better bring me something better than a fuckin myth. And soon!" He ended.

The chief turned and exited the room, leaving all of

them in stunned silence and confusion. As he left, the people in the room began talking and everyone knew of the same rumors. These Four Horsemen were out to eliminate the street competition.

*** *** *** *** ***

By the time Rich finished briefing his boys on what to expect, even he'd begun to re-assess his view of this Four Horsemen threat. At first he thought this nigga Chalice was just trying to scare everybody up before he made his move. But now it seemed that there might be more to it. He wasn't really scared, not really. He just didn't know who was going to be next. All he knew for sure was that Chalice wiped Paint's whole crew out in a single day and he took his business from him. Which was why Rich stepped up security at his car lots. He had a trick for them niggas if they tried something stupid.

*** *** *** *** ***

"So you and Cujo from Miami too?" Chalice asked.

At the moment he and Paris were walking up the street away from the hotel they were staying at.

"Nah, we lived down here once, for about two years. We're originally from North Carolina," Paris said.

"Oh yeah. Where about?" Chalice asked. "I've got some people throughout the Carolinas."

They stopped at one of the stores. Chalice got a bottle water while Paris get a coke.

"I was born in Gastonia NC. It's about the same as Augusta, but we started to move around when I was about eight. So I've seen a lot of places," Paris explained.

They ended up in an area that was a park, in a sense.

There were people on skates and roller blades. Chalice found a bench and they sat down. "So tell me," he started. "What do you know about these Miami King Pins?"

"Depends on which ones you deal with," Paris began. "The local niggas who have a connect are usually some bullshit when it comes to out of state niggas. Those will be the one's trying to rob you. The Jamaicans and Dominicans do good business, but they've got some funny ways about them. You don't want to mess with the Haitians at all, them niggas is stupid." Paris paused to let that sink it. "The Columbians, those are some big time muthafuckas. You fuck with them, you make some big money. The Cubans are alright too, but not as big as the Cartel. Down here the Cartel is more powerful than the Italian or Irish Mafia in New York and that's powerful!"

Chalice nodded his head. He knew that Paris had heard Erica tell him that this guy Joker was a bastard Columbian. From the way she explained it, Joker's mother had been full blooded Columbian, but she'd come to America to attend college. Here she met a black man and became pregnant. When her father found out and learned that she was going to have the child, he dispatched some of his men. They ended up killing the baby's father by accident. They were only told to teach him a lesson. But got carried away.

Joker was born and raised in South Miami, which was considered the ghettos and slums. His Grandfather didn't even acknowledge his existence until he was 16 years of age when some renegade Cubans had come to break into their house and Joker had used a knife to cut one. The killing was bad enough that his mother had to ask her father to step in and stop the war that was about to start. The Cubans assumed Joker was black. At which point his grandfather took notice of him. He even took Joker to South America to live and learn for six years. Although Joker wasn't a full blooded cartel, he was designated a front man and had all of the support he needed.

Joker had also learned the art of killing. The part of the story that hadn't been told about the Cubans coming to rob them, was that they'd come to rape his mother. By the time Joker was awakened, two of them had already violated her. He killed the third while the first two fled. Out of shame, his mother made him promise never to tell her father. So when Joker returned to Miami six years later, he finished what he started.

*** *** *** *** ***

The meeting took place in what looked to be a marina boating dock of sorts, Chalice wasn't exactly sure. But on that day, at exactly 10:45pm, he stood in front of the Mercedes Bens with Paris next to him. Both Erica and Pumpkin sat in the front seat of the car with the doors open.

That was the scene when the four Range Rovers pulled into the lot directly in front of them, about ten feet away. The high beam head lights were still on as the man and woman stepped out of the second truck.

Chalice watched as they paused to speak with the guys in the first truck. Then he heard Erica and Pumpkin get out. Both he and Paris kept their silence as Erica and Pumpkin met the brown skinned Blackman and the slightly lighter women, halfway. It was then that Chalice realized the woman was actually a girl about the same age as Pumpkin. In fact, once Erica hugged her and kissed her on the cheek, both Pumpkin and the girl pulled off to the side to talk while Erica and the man walked back to the Mercedes.

"Chalice, I'd like you to meet Joker, who also happens to be Pumpkins Godfather. That's his daughter, Princess. Joker, this is Chalice and Pumpkins' boyfriend Paris," Erica explained.

Chalice stuck his hand out while at the same time he

noticed the slight traces of gray in the older man's hair. He guessed that Joker was about 45, maybe older. "Nice to meet you," Chalice said. He watched as Joker smiled, shook his hand and then he shook Paris' hand.

"It's so good to finally meet you," Joker told him with a slightly husky voice. "Erica has told me quite a lot about you. Since your son carries the same name as my family, we seem to have a lot in common."

"Oh, I forgot to tell him," Erica put in. "Giavoni is the actual name of Joker's family. Their last name, which makes it the Giavoni Cartel."

Chalice nodded. Now understanding the name better. "She's explained some things to me," Chalice began to tell him. "Not any secrets, but enough to know what to expect business wise."

"True, true," Joker smiled. "But did she tell you how I became the Joker?"

"Nah, I didn't hear that."

Joker laughed. "It's simple really. People started calling me that because I usually laugh when I get mad and I laugh harder when I inflict pain on my enemies."

Chalice thought about that. "Well, let's just see if we can be friends. I've got enough enemies to worry about as it is," he told Joker.

"This wouldn't happen to be the situation that started a little over a year ago would it?" Joker asked. He watched as Chalice nodded.

He knew the Joker was aware of the robbery. After all, he'd fronted Erica the dope to get back on.

"I offered to let my enforcer, Black Smoke, come and correct that problem. But...," he paused and looked at Erica. "It would seem that Erica here thinks that you're..., uh..., built like Pumpkins father use to be. My ex-partner and those are some pretty big shoes to fill my friend."

"I don't know about filling any shoes," Chalice told him.

"I didn't know Pumpkin's old man, but what I do know is those people who violated, they will be dealt with. You can believe in that."

Joker nodded several times as he spoke, he could see what Erica saw in Chalice, even if he were young in age. He really wanted to see how this young man handled his problem.

Later that night. Both of their rooms were on the seventh floor of the hotel, which also had a balcony. Paris usually kept a lot of his thoughts to himself and held his tongue until it was time to speak. He found Chalice standing out on the balcony smoking a cigarette.

"Deep into your thoughts hu?" Paris said.

"Something like that," Chalice returned. There wasn't any need to ask why he wasn't with Pumpkin, since she was sharing a room with Erica and the men were sharing.

"Have you decided how you wanted to put down when we get home?" Paris asked.

He knew that they'd only been expecting to buy 12 kilo's on this trip. What none of them had expected was for Joker to give Chalice a gift of friendship since his son was named after them. But Joker had given them an extra eight kilos with no return on it.

"Honestly...." Chalice hit the cigarette. "I'm thinking about going big. But then there's two problems outside of that little beef."

"I know the cops are one. So what's the other?" Paris asked.

Chalice was quiet for a while, thinking carefully before his thoughts became words. "This is my first time selling dope. I've never been a dope boy. So in truth, I'm expecting to make some mistakes. But the mistakes I don't want to make are the ones that can be avoided."

"In other words," Paris added. "You don't want to do something that will bring unwanted attention."

93

Erica had been putting down for years and she'd never gotten hot. She never went out there real big. There wasn't any need to. The bigger you went the more attention you got.

"The cop situation I can probably get around," Chalice stated. "It shouldn't be too hard to find some crooked cops and plug in. You know, you've still got to be smart even with that. But if we jump out there and go real big, then we've got other big dealers to worry about. Like that nigga Mustafa out in Barton Village and that nigga Cory, up on the Hill. And the snitches, those are the real problems."

They were both silent in thought. Trying to figure out how to deal with all of that. Neither Mustafa nor Cory were going to be a small situation to deal with.

"Man," Paris said. "All I can say is, I'm down wit' you bruh. Big or small problems, we can solve them together. You just let me know what I need to do and it's done."

Trai'Quan

Chapter Eleven

Four men, all dressed in black outfits and black ski masks were timing the security guard that patrolled the car lot. Using silent hand signals, one flashed a message to another, which he must've been read because he got up and ran down the street then crouched down as if he really didn't want to be seen. The other three watched as he eventually came up to the car lot then paused, stooped down and appeared to wait. The guard came around again whistling Dixie, which wasn't unusual, since he was a big red neck.

As he unsuspectingly walked over to the last car and began to pass it, the three men across the street watched as the figure in black snuck up with something shiny, which gleamed in his hand. The hand with the object snaked around the guard's throat and then there was a brief struggle before they watched the dark figure drag the guard behind one of the cars.

A moments silence went by and then the figure reappeared once again. This time he flashed some hand signs and the other three made their way across the street. When they got there, one broke away from the group and ran over to the big 18 wheel car carrier, which was capable of carrying 12 cars at once, while the others went over to the building. One of them stooped down to inspect the door locks and alarm key pad. Then after a minute he began to take the cover off the alarm and proceeded to clip wires. Next, he pulled out two pieces of metal which he placed into the locks. Soon there was a click and the door opened. At that same time they heard the truck start up.

*** *** *** *** ***

Both Chalice and Erica were standing in the parking lot

of the used car lot that they had just bought. They'd been talking when the truck with the 12 cars loaded on it, pulled up. It stopped directly in front of them and one man, still dressed in black, jumped from the passenger seat.

He ran over to them and asked, "Where do you want em?"

Chalice looked at Paris, then past him to the truck. John-John had been driving and he'd guessed that they left Que and B' Nice at the lot. "Shit, we ain't got but ten cars on this whole lot. It really don't matter where you put em. But yo..., how many more trips y'all gone make tonight?" He asked.

They were standing in front of Erica's Q.5, as she leaned on the hood, doing her nails. She was wearing a thigh length, denim skirt, with a blouse and a Carolina Panthers, Starter jacket.

"It won't take but two and a half more trips, then we can turn it in for tonight, unless you've got something else you want to get into," Paris stated.

"Nah, I'll see you at the house and we'll go over those other plans for Rugar's Pool halls and bar. Before y'all split up. Let the guys know there's a Bar-B-Que at our house Saturday," Chalice said.

Paris said goodbye to Erica and agreed to take a message back for Pumpkin. Then he went back to the truck and got in. As he was leaving, Erica was wondering what he was going to do when Pumpkin went to college in a few more months. She was sending her daughter to Atlanta so that she could attend Spellman University.

On the way back home Erica told Chalice, "I've got three more girls to dance at your club, that is, if you've got room."

Chalice was just about to answer, when they stopped at a red light and something caught his attention. "Baby, you got your twins on you?" He asked.

Extended Clip

At first Erica started to ask why, but for some reason she didn't. Instead, she picked up her pocket book and pulled out both nickel plated 9mm's and checked the clips. There wasn't any need to ask if he had the .44s because he never left home without them.

"Now, you wanna tell me what's up?" She asked.

She watched him look into the side mirror as the light changed. "There's a car back there that's been with us on every turn we've made and for the past four blocks. It's the same blue Cadillac," he explained.

Erica looked in the rearview mirror and saw the car. Since she was driving, she should've seen it before he did. She made a point of turning onto another street then drove slowly. But the other car kept going.

"Baby you might just be paranoid," she said.

"You just stay on point. It ain't over yet," he replied. Chalice didn't tell her that he'd begun getting one of those migraine headaches as soon as he noticed the car. For some reason he knew something was up.

Erica drove in silence for couple of blocks and was about to stop at a stop sign, when all of a sudden the blue Cadillac pulled up in front of them and blocked the street. Before either one of them could do anything, two men stepped from the car holding what looked like Uzi's or Mack 10's, which they both brought up and took aim with.

"Duck!" Chalice screamed.

Erica's foot pressed down on the brake and she threw the Q5 into park at about the same time the windshield exploded.

"Yeah..., yeah...! You weak muthafuckas act like you hard now! Come on..., act a fool!" The guy screamed.

Chalice looked across at Erica. "That's Paint and whoever the other nigga is. I'm gone get Paint, you get that nigga!" He instructed.

"Yeah Daddy! It's been a while since I've had this kind

98

of fun!" Erica responded.

They waited, thinking the niggas would have to change clips sooner or later. This wasn't a movie, even with extended clips they had to stop shooting at some point. Then, suddenly, there was silence.

"A'ight, let's get it!" Chalice yelled.

Paint was caught off guard when the doors opened on both sides. He looked over at Bruce. They were both changing clips, but not fast enough. "Oh shit!" He exclaimed as the first shots rang out.

"Pop.... Pop.... Pop...."

Chalice turned and broke out into a run. He wasn't sure if the nigga he was after was Paint or that other nigga but he hoped that it was Paint. They still had some unfinished business to take care of.

Erica could tell that she'd hit the nigga she was following with one of her shots because of the way his shoulder sagged as he ran. She tried to shorten the distance between them as they entered the parking lot of some business. She leaned her body forward slightly then picked up the pace, but it seemed like the nigga started to run a little faster or something.

When he reached the end of the lot and turned the corner of the building, Bruce thought that he'd gotten away. He looked around for a place to hide then his eyes landed on the dumpster. Using what was left of his strength he made his way over to it, lifted the top and then climbed inside.

Erica turned the corner only ten seconds later and stopped dead in her tracks. The alley where she now stood was quite long. She couldn't see this nigga getting to the end of it that fast, yet she didn't see him anywhere. She wasn't stupid. *'That punk hiding,'* she thought.

She slowed down to a walk and made it a point to look inside, as well as under, a couple of cars on the side of the alley. She didn't see anything so she kept moving. The whole time she's looking around and asking herself, *'If I was a coward, where would I hide?'* She was just about to bypass the set of dumpsters when the thought came to her. Erica paused in step and considered it. *'Nah, the nigga can't be that desperate,'* she told herself.

Just when the thought set in and she was about to walk off, Erica heard a low, muzzled sneeze come from one of the dumpsters.

"Son of a bitch!" She said. She checked both of her guns and saw that she still had something in the clips then walked over to the one that the sneeze came from. She wasn't worried about the nigga shooting her because she'd passed the Tech he was carrying on the side of the street, a little while back. That is, unless he had another gun.

She lifted the top of the dumpster and there he was, covered in trash and dirty himself. She didn't hesitate, but aimed and squeeze both triggers.

Inside the graveyard a couple of blocks over, Chalice stepped up to a large head stone. He was looking at a big pile of dirt a couple graves over. He would've overlooked the area except his eye caught sight of it. He thought to himself, *'If this nigga did that..., he must want to live real bad.'* The mental picture he got in his mind nearly made him laugh. Either way, Chalice slowly moved over and looked down into the hollow cavity of the earth.

What he saw really did make him laugh. Paint wasn't only inside the grave, he was down on his knees with his head bowed forward in prayer. On the ground in front of him was the empty Uzi and what looked like an old crack pipe. It was hard for him to stop laughing, but Chalice eventually got the strength to bring both .44, nickel plated twins up to aim.

He cocked his head and thought he heard some of what the nigga was saying. "Please, Jesus, Moses, Abraham. Hell, even Muhammad. Somebody, don't let this nigga kill me."

"Damn bruh," Chalice said as he watched Paint's eyes open and look into the barrel of both guns. "I know this ain't the answer you might have been looking for, but you been lookin for God in all the wrong places," Chalice told him as he squeezed both triggers. He watched as Paint's body did a dance, the dance niggas do right before their soul's left their bodies. Chalice didn't feel any type of remorse, especially with the crack pipe down there on the ground in front of the loser.

"Damn," he said as the sound of the gun shots faded into silence. "Now I get it." He looked down at Paint's body as if it was about to answer. "Must've been trying to get to hell and not Heaven," he laughed. "Cause that's definitely where yo lame ass going."

*** *** *** *** ***

"Son of a bitch!" Rich screamed.

He'd just stepped out of his Benz in front of the car lot after he received a call 45 minutes ago. He had been in bed, sleeping good. Having fucked Tina real good. The last thing he expected was to get a call from that nigga Paris.

"Uh, Hello?" Rich had asked.

"That boy Rich nigga. What up boy."

He looked at the clock. It read 5:45am. "Man, who the fuck is this? Nigga, it's too early to be playing on the phone," Rich complained.

Tina rolled over. "Baby are you alright?"

But Rich hushed her up.

"Nigga this P," the voice had become serious.

"P...? Who, Paint?" Rich asked.

"Nah nigga. This Paris, the real P nigga. But yo, I was just calling to tell you that somebody been by your car lot and the shit ain't pretty."

That call had been 30 minutes ago. Now Rich stood looking at his lot. "How the fuck, did a nigga just up and steal 42 cars?" He banged his fist on the hood of the Benz then turned and looked at the two cars that had been left behind. One was a used Chevy, the other was a new Volvo. Pinned to the windshield of the Chevy was a piece of paper.

Rich walked over to the car, snatched the paper down and read it...

"Something old, something new."
The Four Horsemen.

Rich balled the paper up and shouted, "If I don't get that ass before the cops do!" Then he turned and made his way to the office. He needed to make a call, if they hadn't stolen that too. It was about time to do something about this shit! "I'm a build my own team. I'm a call em 'The Regulators'. Yeah, that's what's up!" He said to himself.

Trai'Quan

Chapter Twelve

"The soul that is sinning shall die. A son himself will not bear nothing because of the error of the father and a father himself will not bear nothing because of the error of the son...."
-Ezekiel 18:20

Two Weeks Later

When the word got out about the Regulators, it hit the streets as if it were on National TV. Mostly because they'd gone out of the way to really put the word out and the fact that their targets were the Four Horsemen. The message was that they were an endangered species.

But the Four Horsemen must've missed that part because they sat around the table in Chalice's private club and laughed at most of it.

"I say we go over to Southside and regulate that ass," B' Nice laughed.

"Yeah, I'm down wit' that," John-John added.

"Me too, them niggas don't bleed Kool-Aid," Que stated, adding his three cents.

Both Chalice and Paris sat there in silence. Chalice, because he'd been thinking and Paris because he was waiting on Chalice to finish thinking and make a decision. The whole situation had been up for debate over the past two weeks, while Rich was making it known that he was indeed a threat. The only reason he hadn't come after the cars was because all of them had been stolen and switched over by him first. Chalice along with Que had re-switched them again. So neither side could take the chance of bringing the cops in.

"This is what we gone do." Chalice sat forward with both arms on the table top. "First of all, I want all four of you to go over to those pool halls and deliver a message to the cats who run them. Then stop by the bar and pay your respects. Let em know that if they don't pay their dues, they don't do business," he paused to see that they understood. "Don't leave without them dues. That's by any means necessary. Damn," Chalice paused.

"What?" Paris asked.

"I always wanted to say that Malcolm X shit. But I thought it would be on some black power shit.... Anyway, it's about time we mount up. Paris, you're in charge." He wasn't worried about them accepting Paris as leader, even at his age, the younger man commanded a whole lot of respect and he didn't take no shit.

*** *** *** *** ***

Rugar got the word about what was going down a little later than everybody else. It was mostly because he was back and forth to DC, but by the time it got to him, Paint had turned up dead. The sad part about it was that on top of everything, he'd died a broke crackhead.

Then he heard the shit about Rich and his, so-called Regulators, who were supposed to be after these Four Horsemen. His boys, Tommy Bird and Roe Dogg had told him about the Four Horsemen earlier, but like them, he'd thought that it had been an inside joke. Even when they made the move on East Boundry. Now he was trying to figure out where he fit into this shit.

*** *** *** *** ***

The outside of the pool hall was fairly full. So much so that when the first man came through the door, no one seemed to be aware of him. A couple minutes later another one came in and went to the bar, where he ordered a beer. In almost no time, all four of them were inside and no one was the wiser.

On one of the tables there was a high stakes game going on. Two guys were playing and another one stood next to the table, holding the money.

When the first shot from the shotgun was fired, it sounded like a bomb went off. Everybody, except the four men, went down to the floor. The guy behind the bar made a move like he was about to reach under the counter, but before he could pull anything, Paris had one of his Glock 9mm's aimed at his head.

"Calm down ole man. Don't make me have to bless you!" He stated.

The old man dropped his hand and his shoulder sagged. John-John pumped two more rounds from the Mossberg into the roof, while Que covered the door. One nigga over behind a table, directly behind Que, had been about to do something stupid. He'd eased out his .38 and was about to take aim at Que's back, not really paying attention to the fact that Que himself wasn't worried, since he wasn't the only one standing.

B' Nice peeped the move and when the nigga took aim, moving with the speed of a cat, B' Nice pulled the sawed off, double barrel from under his trench coat and squeezed both triggers. The noise was almost enough to make a body go deaf as the two shells left the barrels and went into the man's body, lifting him off the ground. It threw him into the far wall, leaving a large hole in side of his chest area.

Silence followed as B' Nice removed the spent shells and put in two new ones.

"Alright people, we ain't got but five minutes and here's what's gone happen in that time. Each one of you is gone walk by the guy with the big book bag. As you walk by, you will put your money inside the bag. Start getting it out now, if he thinks your shitting him…, well, you saw what he just did wit' that shot gun," Paris explained. Then, as an afterthought, he turned to the bartender. "Aye ole man, this here's a hold up. Go ahead and empty your registers too. Please don't try nothing stupid," he instructed and then paused to smile. "Oh, by the way. In case any of you ain't put the pieces together yet, standing before you is what's called, The Four Horsemen."

Nobody gave them anymore trouble, they all began doing as he'd instructed, without question. At one point Paris thought that B' Nice was going to draw down on a woman because she only seemed to have $10, which she pulled out of her bra. But he didn't. Instead, he took the ten and made her move to the other side of the room.

Once they finished, Paris spoke again. "Now all of you can thank yo boy Rugar. Had he paid his upfront business dues, you wouldn't have to be bothered like this. Honestly, the Four Horsemen sure do appreciate your donations."

Then, just as quickly and smoothly, the four men filed out of the Pool hall one by one, each getting into a different car before pulling off. People watched from the windows, but no one seemed to notice the cocaine white Escalade.

Chalice looked at the time on his watch, they were two minutes over. But then again this was the last Pool hall, they'd already hit the first two and still had the bar. He started the truck and just as he pulled away from the curb, two Police cars came down the street, lights flashing and all.

He hadn't been worried about that either, he'd heard each call on the police scanner he had. Since each pool hall was spaced out, they seemed to be running all over the city. Never the less, everything was going like he expected. He guessed that Rugar would be in a blind rage when he finally got the news and while Rugar would be preparing himself for a hit, it would be Rich that they went after next. Rich thought that he was safe, but he wasn't.

*** *** *** *** ***

"Hell No!" Rugar screamed. "I ain't going for it."

He'd just received word that all three of his Pool halls and his bar, had been robbed. The Four Horsemen's name was ringing loud. Rugar made his mind up, he wasn't about to take it lying down like a bitch. He was gone strike back.

"Don't that bitch own the strip club down on Broad Street? The one that's got something goin on this weekend?" He asked, talking to Tommy Bird and Roe Dogg. Both of them were sitting in front of him.

"Yeah, I believe so. Why?" Tommy asked.

"Listen Ru...," Roe Dogg spoke up. "You know security gone be tight at that joint. Not only is Cujo gone be on it, but you know he got a few cops who patrol it too, especially when they do something big."

Rugar took a moment to think about it. He had to re-think the whole idea. "I want y'all get some more boys and watch that joint. If you see a chance to hit this nigga without being caught..., then please, make me happy," he told them, thinking, that there was no way in hell that he was about to let this go unanswered.

*** *** *** *** ***

Erica curled up on the couch in Chalice's arms as they watched a movie that she'd rented. Neither one of them were really paying any attention to the movie, they were too busy trying to get their feel on.

"Hey, we'll be back!" Pumpkin called out.

But as she did, Chalice turned his head to look back at her. "Hold up, stole up. Where you think y'all going? It's almost late," he said.

"There's this movie at the cinema exchange that I wanna catch. It starts at 9:30 and Paris is gone take me to see it," Pumpkin explained.

"Oh yeah? Where Paris at?" He asked.

"… Uh. Outside in his truck," she told him.

The whole time Erica didn't say anything. Giavoni was asleep in his playpen right there in the room with them. There really wasn't any reason she couldn't go, but she left it up to Chalice.

"A'ight," he gave in. "So this movie gone be over about 11:30 or so. Tell Paris I said respectable young women don't hang out late, so have that ass back in this house by 12:30."

"12:30?" Pumpkin asked.

"What, you think you can make it back by 11:45?" He asked.

"Ugh. No. 12:30 will do," she said. Then added, "Thanks Daddy."

"No problem."

Erica laughed as Pumpkin made her way outside, but as soon as Pumpkin was gone, he started kissing her again.

"Hey, hey. You ain't got to be spitting on me," she said.

"Oh yeah, I'm gone spit on somebody and since Giavoni asleep...,"

"Uh.... But I've been meaning to ask you, with all of this going on with Rugar and Rich. What are you going to do with all of the dope?" She asked.

Because he hadn't started moving the dope yet, Chalice had really been focused on dealing with these three chumps first. "We gone get to it. Right now we just trying to get all of the road kill out of the streets. Once these other two niggas is dealt with, then we can do that," he explained.

What he didn't tell her, was that he suspected they might have problems with Mustafa or Cory, maybe both. At the same time, from what he could find out, Mustafa was on some real Frank White, 'King of New York' shit. If he found out that niggas were moving some real big shit, he would try to muscle his way in on their business. Cory wasn't as aggressive as Mustafa, but some said that Cory was shiesty. They even went as far as to say Cory would put the cops on you if you were stepping on his toes. How true that was, he didn't know.

"Still trying to figure out what to do about these other niggas," he said.

"Barton Village and Sand Hills?" She asked.

Erica already knew what the main problem was. She didn't exactly know the details, but she'd overheard part of the conversation Chalice had with Cujo about it. From what she did get, Cujo thought those two would be more of a problem than Paint, Rich and Rugar.

*** *** *** *** ***

"Na, boy, come again...."

Rich sighed as Big Afrika asked him to repeat what he had just explained. It hadn't been his intention to let Big Afrika know about his local troubles, but when the King pin asked why he hadn't come down to Jacksonville to get the drop he asked for, Rich had to tell him something.

"It ain't all that serious bruh," Rich told him. "It's just some unfinished shit me and my team should have seen about. But since we slipped on it, we've got this nigga running around robbing and killing folks," Rich told him. But he wasn't really telling Big Afrika everything. Mostly because he didn't want to look weary himself. When he'd first met Big Afrika, Rich had given off the impression that he was really a big issue in Augusta.

"Yo, all I'm saying is this," Big Afrika told him over the phone. "I've got a nice size team of niggas right there in Jacksonville. It won't take but a phone call and they'll be on the way up there. All you gotta do is ask."

That was the problem, he'd already figured out that Big Afrika was on some mob shit. If he let him come in to help, Big Afrika was going to use him as a door way in. He'd begin to move more of his people into the city and then before he knew it, he wouldn't be buying from Big Afrika, he'd be working for Big Afrika.

"Nah bruh..., I got it. The shit'll be over in about a week or two. Then I'm a get that," Rich told him.

The call didn't last much longer after that. Once he hung up, Rich was seriously trying to figure out how he could end this problem. He knew how, he just had to do it.

Chapter Thirteen

The Moment of Truth

Rich didn't exactly know how to take it, three days had passed and not a word had been heard from the Four Horsemen. He knew they hadn't just fallen off the face of the planet. Something had to be up.

It was a Saturday morning and he'd just woke up. He pulled his arm from under Tina's head and began to get out of bed. His mind thought, *'For a white girl, the bitch sure had a hell of a fuck game.'* He walked into the bathroom and turned the shower on, tested the water and then took his pajamas off to step into it.

His mind drifted back to Chalice. The nigga thought that he'd done some damage by pulling those cars off the lot. All he'd done was cause him to have the same niggas go out a steal some more and switched them over.

"Yeah, the nigga thought he had me down bad. You can't hurt steel baby," he laughed and then thought, *'Maybe that was why I hadn't heard anything. Maybe the nigga realized I couldn't be hurt.'*

*** *** *** *** ***

9:30am.

When Chalice woke up, the day was just getting started. He realized that he was in bed alone but didn't trip it. After getting up he found that there wasn't anything telling where she and Pumpkin had gone. It was Saturday, they might've gone shopping.

As he headed for the shower his mind was focused. He'd already told himself that tonight was the last night he'd have to worry about these niggas. By the end of it, all hell was going to break loose. The only thing was, he really didn't want to take Erica with him when he set out to do his thing. Since his team would be doing their own thing, he didn't have anyone else to watch his back.

Either way, that was for later. Today he had to go over to his club around noon to make sure that everything would be ready for tonight's opening. He couldn't afford any fuck ups, he had too much money invested into the club and until he started hustling the dope, that money didn't have any back up yet.

Which also brought him to thoughts of the hustle. Both Paris and Que said that they could handle Mustafa and Cory. He didn't exactly know what that meant, but it sounded like if push came to shove, they were going to do what they do. That could mean a war. He had to put some more thought into that.

*** *** *** *** ***

11:01AM

Rugar normally had a slow start to his day. It never really got started until around noon, even with some help. That was why he still stood at his island bar with a razor in his hand, which he used to chop up the white powder, then divide it. He pulled out a roll of money and peeled off a hundred. He rolled it up and put one end to his nose, with the other near the coke. He snorted one line, switched nostrils and then snorted the other line. When he finished, he held his head back for the drain.

Now his day was started. *'What am I gone do today?'* He thought. *'Should I plot on how to kill this nigga, or should I continue to focus on my money?'* As of late, Rugar hadn't been having his hands on in his business affairs. He'd left everything up to Tommy Bird. The money still came through like it was supposed to, but he just hadn't been in the mood to go out much. He hadn't even been over to see that lil bitch Kim, who he'd been trying to fuck.

It wasn't as if he were scared. Nah, he wasn't scared to go out, there was just too much going on out there. Either way he wasn't trying to let this nigga Chalice, catch him slipping. Rugar had finally realized that these niggas were playing for keeps.

There hadn't been any word about the Four Horsemen yet. Rugar wondered if them niggas had been picked up by the cops or something. But that shit would have been in the news. Nah, they were just waiting on something. But what? He thought that by now they would have been back to the pool halls, which was why he'd put some extra men, who wouldn't be scared to shoot back, in them. Maybe they expected him to do that. *'Yeah,'* he thought. *'That's what it is.'*

*** *** *** *** ***

1:21pm

The police chief sat in his office, thinking. He'd been looking over the reports and statements concerning these Four Horsemen. He had looked at what his people had been doing since they appeared. Next, he looked at the reports from the past three days. He'd been doing all of this for the past day and a half now. He had a bad feeling. He'd been a cop long enough to know the patterns were wrong somewhere. He couldn't say where, it was just something he knew in his guts. The past few days had been too quiet, not a word from these guys. His people had been working extra hard, looking for connections but thus far, only two names came up. Richard Brown and Lester Dickerson. AKA, Rich and Rugar.

There would've been three, but they'd recovered the body of a guy they called Paint. Found him in the graveyard sometime back. By now the sister had the body. She hadn't even shed a tear over him and the chief knew why. Some snitch had informed them that these were the three who robbed her and the boyfriend some time back. The boyfriend had come out of his coma, then all this shit started.

He'd had his people look into them, but they couldn't find anything that connected them to the death. He certainly didn't think the sister was one of these Four Horsemen. From what he understood, they were all men and their alibis were good.

Maybe he was missing something. The cases were unsolved that was for sure. But he could still feel it, these Four Horsemen were about to do something and whatever it was, there would be a lot of bodies when the smoke cleared.

*** *** *** *** ***

4:30pm

At first Rich started not to come, but he'd changed his mind. He didn't think that they would be stupid enough to try anything in broad day light. Plus, here in Southside, he was like a king pin. These were his streets and everybody knew it. On top of that, he had his Regulators out in the streets. That was how Rich found himself sitting on the hood of his Benz, talking to a hood rat named Keisha.

"Nigga, I thought you was scared to come out of the house or something. You ain't been out here in a minute," Keisha said.

"Bitch don't play wit' me. Why the fuck would I be scared to come out?" Rich asked.

"Well," she laughed. "From the way I hear it, the Four Horsemen ain't exactly playing with the PlayStation. Niggas said you been on ice since they got Paint and that

115

crackhead Bruce," Keisha told him.

Rich thought about it. *'This bitch trying to see how hard a nigga is. She thinking a nigga gone bow down to these niggas.'* "Well, even if that was true, since my Regulators done came about, I ain't heard shit from these, so called, Four Horsemen. So they must not be all that. Them niggas ain't about this life," he stated.

"Mmm hmm, I bet," she replied. "Them niggas you running around here calling themselves Regulators, ain't but the same ole beer drinking, dumb ass niggas, out here in the streets every day. They ain't regulating shit but a 40 Oz, or double duce," she laughed.

"Oh, excuse me. Let me get that." They watched as a bum reached between them to pick up a can and add it to the ones in his bag.

"You know what I think," she started back. "I think them Four Horsemen niggas are just sitting back, watching to see if yo boys really 'bout that Life'. In fact, I wouldn't be surprised if they was out here watching y'all now," she said. She smiled at the old dirty bum as he waved, on his way up the side walk.

Rich was so caught up in what she said that he didn't even see the wink of the eye that the old man gave her. So what if the Regulators didn't do nothing but hang around the hood? He'd made sure that they all had guns now and he didn't think that they would just let niggas rush up in his spot.

Then his thoughts shifted, he looked at the way Keisha was wearing the little wrap around Tennis skirt. *'Nah, better not do that,'* he thought.

*** *** *** *** ***

B' Nice started up the car then he looked at the time on his watch, ten minutes to five. He still had to swing around the other side and pick Chalice up. Putting the car in drive, he pulled off, leaving the gas station and turning the corner. Getting onto Old Savannah, he drove down by the projects. There were a number of niggas standing outside, hustling as if nothing would ever happen. *'Yeah,'* he thought. *'These niggas are too comfortable and laid back, which will end up being their down fall.'*

He slowed down, looking for Chalice. He spotted the old man limping up the street, picking up cans. The man's clothing made him look as if he was indeed homeless, with a coat that had patches on it and pants that looked a size too big for him, as if he'd just lost some weight. From inside the Hummer that B' Nice was driving, he could see the old man's face and even that looked dirty. Still, he turned the Hummer over to the side walk and let the passenger side window down.

"Say ole man, you need a ride?"

There'd been a woman walking with her two kids and when she overheard the question, she twisted her face up, somewhat discussed at the looks of the old man.

"Shit. If you going round by the junk yard, yeah I could use a lift," The grimy voice said.

The woman kept walking as the old man opened the door and got inside, trash bag with the cans in it and all.

B' Nice put the hummer into drive and pulled off. Neither one of them spoke a word. Then after he turned off of Old Savannah, going through Grand Boulevard, they spoke.

"So what's up?" B' Nice asked.

The old man reached up and turned the rearview mirror so that he could look into it. Then he began to peal the fake hair off his chin. "Shit, this fuckin beard itches like hell." Now the voice had changed, it wasn't grimy, it was Chalice's voice. He then removed the beard and he looked ten years younger. "Yeah, them niggas sleepin. I must've

117

stood three feet away from that nigga Rich and a girl named Keisha as they talked and she tried to tell him," Chalice laughed. "Dumb ass nigga, thinking them Regulator niggas is the reason why the Four Horsemen ain't moved on em yet."

"Yeah, imagine that," B' Nice laughed too.

"Look, I got something special I want you to do when y'all move," Chalice said.

Chalice explained as B' Nice continued to drive and listen. He nodded his head, while in his own mind, B' Nice was admitting that this nigga Chalice, really did know what the fuck he was doing. Seriously, who else would have dressed up like a bum picking up cans and stood three feet away from the nigga he was out to kill? Classic.

*** *** *** *** ***

6:08pm

Having changed clothes and taken a good bath, both Chalice and Erica were inside their room getting dressed. She sat on the bed and pulled on her black, Nike cross trainers. Tonight she was wearing a pair of Apple bottom jeans and a bullet proof vest with a T-shirt over it. Erica slipped both of the shoulder holsters on, one under her right arm, the other under the left. She picked up each of her 9mm's and checked the clips. She pushed them into the holsters and then put the two extra clips in her pockets. She lifted the pistol grip Mossberg, nickel plated 20 gauge pump and slid shells into its chamber.

While she was doing that, Chalice put his vest and two holsters on. He put the .44 Desert Eagles into them and slipped his two clips in his pockets. He then picked up the Black Rain, AR-15 with its clip.

Then, together, they both pulled on the black jackets they had to conceal the guns they wore.

"Check your watch before we leave. I've got 6:17pm," he told her.

"Hold up." She adjusted hers. "6:18?"

"Time!" He called out. Which meant that they were both on the same time.

Before the left the room, they picked up the two duffle bags that had their change of clothing in them. They didn't want to walk up into the club wearing the shit they wore on the lick, that wouldn't make any sense. He had Erica book a motel room earlier.

Chalice had thought the whole thing through, which was exactly why he'd set everything up over the past three days. He'd also made it a point to have Pumpkin, Shae and two other motel rooms on standby. All of them were across town, a long way from where the action was about to take place.

*** *** *** *** ***

Inside of the back room of the car lot that Chalice and Erica owned. The four men were doing almost the exact same thing. Their assortment of guns consisted of four pump 12 gage shotguns and four nine millimeters, with six in all clips that held 17 rounds. They also had shoulder holsters and vests to go with everything else.

Paris had a hard time convincing Chalice that they might need the vest on this job. Especially since he would be taking Erica with him. He still didn't fully understand that, except for the fact that it seemed Erica used to be in the streets like that, back in her day.

"It's 6:19pm. Everybody check your watches. Put one minute ahead. Start with Paris, then Que, then John-John," B' Nice said.

"Time...," Paris said.

"Time...," Que checked in.

"Time...," John-John added.

They were all on point.

"A'ight. At approximately 7:33, the show gone start. Until then, let's make sure we don't do nothing stupid."

Trai'Quan

Chapter Fifteen

"I'm so tied up on my own, I'm so tired of being alone, won't you help me girl.... Just as soon as you caaannn...."
-Al Green

Rich couldn't believe that he'd let the bitch trick him but there he was at Keisha's house, over on 8th and Grand. He'd already fucked her once. It hadn't been his intension to fuck her, but shit, free pussy is free pussy. Either way, he lay back in her bed, naked, waiting on the bitch to finish in the bathroom.

One thing he had to admit, the bitch had a fool doggy style on her. He hadn't been in the pussy a good 15 minutes when she pulled the first nut up out of him.

He glanced over at the clock and saw that it read 7:29. *'I might just make this lil bitch my second wife or something,'* Rich thought. But then again she had three kids and he damn sure wasn't about to be no step-daddy to nobody else's kids. He wasn't really selfish, but he had too much going on to be dealing with kids. That's why he prayed Tina didn't end up being pregnant.

*** *** *** *** ***

Outside in the streets, business was booming. Cats were coming from all over to get the dope, Jue-Jue was even getting a little paranoid thinking that some of these junkies might be undercover Detectives. But the cops wouldn't go through that much trouble to catch some small time hustlers like them.

He saw Baby Chris down the street, along with a couple of the other guys. They were getting good money and since Southside Apartments was only two streets, there weren't but 50 big. It was easy to catch the sales. Shit, everybody in this area sold for the same nigga anyway... Rich.

"S... say J....Jue-Jue.... Let... m...m....me.... get a... d...dime... from you. I'll w...work for it."

Jue-Jue turned to look at the crackhead bitch. Now normally he didn't have any problems with no bitch working for some dope. But this bitch was...., ugh.... She was short, about 5'4 and thin, like 98lbs. Her hair was a mess and at least four of her front teeth were missing. Plus the bitch's face was sunk in like a Pug dog. Ugh!

"Bitch, if you don't get the fuck out of my face. Go on down there and holla at one of them other niggas. They might give you some play," he told her. "But I doubt it. You one ugly ass bitch!" He laughed.

Tears welled up in Kenya's eyes, she knew this nigga didn't remember her as she looked up at him in desperation. She hadn't always been down bad and she wasn't always ugly. Just like she wasn't always a smoker. There had been a time when Kenya was Home Coming Queen at TW Josey High school. At that time, Jue-Jue had gone out of his way to get at her until one day she finally gave in.

Six months later he had her smoke a funny joint, which had been laced with crack. Another six months after that, she was smoking straight crack. Her shape slowly vanished and eventually a trick knocked out her teeth while beating her up. She'd also had two miscarriages, all because of the no good, nigga right in front of her. And now he wouldn't give her none of the same shit he'd turned her onto in the first place.

But she thought he just couldn't remember her. "Nig....ga.... One of these d...days, y...you gone g...get what's c...c...coming to you. W...when that day g...gets here..., y...you ain't gone want it..., y...you gone," she paused because it was hard for her to get the words out. "You... gone... f...f...fold up like a bitch! Yeah, I...ain't

123

psychic b...b...but I c...can sho read yo f...f...future. Believe w...when I tell you...," she looked straight into his smiling face. "God don't like ugly." she said without a stutter. She then spit in his face.

"You stupid bitch!" Jue-Jue roared. Without even thinking, he swung his arm backwards and hit her in the mouth. Next he caught her with a jab and before she fell to the ground, he shot her a quick upper cut, which caused her to fly backwards and spit out two more of her teeth. "Fuck ass hoe!" He shouted.

Jue-Jue wasn't aware of the man walking towards them in the black trench coat. The tail of the coat blew in the wind and he had a stocking cap, rolled up on top of his head.

"Didn't the lady just tell you... that God don't like evil?" The man asked.

Jue-Jue looked up and watched as the nigga walked by him and knelt down next to the crack head to help her up. He watched as she pulled herself together and looked deep into the man's eyes.

"You alright Queen?" He asked.

Still looking into his eyes, she felt a shiver run through her body. What she saw was death. "I...I'm... fine," she stuttered. She watched as he reached into his coat pocket, pulled out two, crisp 100 dollar bills and handed them to her.

"Listen lil sister, if you choose to buy dope wit this, that's your choice. We've all got choices in life, some good, others bad. But either way you look at it, we choose," he paused and gave her a smile. "But if I was you, I'd go buy some food and take it in for tonight. These streets ain't safe..., not tonight they ain't."

Now Jue-Jue was pissed. "Hold the fuck up Malcolm X!" He looked around to see the crackheads face. "Who the fuck is this nigga supposed to be?" He asked.

"God," Kenya replied. "And Lord knows I feel for your

soul."

"The fuck type of shit is that?" Jue-Jue asked.

That's when the man turned to face him and the look that Jue-Jue saw in his eyes struck real fear in him. Just as the turn was completed Jue-Jue watched as he pushed the end of his trench coat out of the way and from under it came the chrome barrel of a .20 gauge Mossberg, pistol grip pump, which was now aimed at his face.

"H...hold up man. I...I don't know who you is, but shit..., I ain't got no beef wit' you. Especially over that crazy bitch," Jue-Jue plead.

"I told you, fold up like a bitch," Kenya said without a stutter.

"Bitch shut the fuck up!" He screamed at her, but he never took his eyes off the gun. If only he could be sure the nigga hadn't put a shell in the chamber. He might be able to get to his .38 and....

"I told you. God don't like ugly!" Kenya chanted but he ignored her.

Jue-Jue damn near fell to his knees. "Man, I...I don't even know who you is. What did I ever do to you?" He asked.

"My name," the man said. "Is Paris Allah and your soul has been forfeited by the Fourth Horsemen.

The sound was like thunder as Kenya flinched. She dropped to her knees before Jue-Jue's body hit the ground and then she heard a series of other shots ringing throughout the projects. "By the mercy of the Lord!" She bowed her head and closed her eyes. "I bare witness that this black man is indeed God in the flesh and I ask for forgiveness from all my sins." But when she opened her eyes, he was gone. She looked around but all she saw was Jue-Jue's headless body shaking on the ground.

Something inside her made her move over and dig into Jue-Jue's pockets. She came up with two thick rolls of money and a Ziploc bag of crack. But even as she looked at the dope, Kenya felt like a big bright light was shining down on her. "Better leave that." She tossed the bag back on the body "I just asked the Lord to forgive me so I'm not smoking no more dope," she told herself and turned to walk off.

People were running scared everywhere she looked. "Oh shit! They killin everybody!" Somebody shouted.

"Hallelujah! Praise God!" She yelled.

*** *** *** *** ***

Baby Chris couldn't believe what he was seeing. They seemed to come from all four corners of the earth and he knew exactly who they were. Now, as he hid behind a car watching the Regulators being murdered, he was scared to death. Thinking that he'd wagged and gotten away, he reached up and wiped the sweat off his forehead. He took a deep breath and that was when he heard the gun cock.

"Where that nigga Rich at?" The voice asked.

The gun was at his head. "Man he at that bitch Keisha's house, 116 8th and Grand. A big yellow house on the corner. Please nigga don't kill me... Please," Baby Chris begged.

"Why should I let you live? After all, you just snitched and sold yo man out." But before Chris could open his mouth to speak. Que had put a slug from the 9mm into the back of his neck and then pumped three more rounds into him before he looked up. He saw a crackhead walking up the street, counting money and talking to herself. "Praise God! Praise the Blackman's God," she sang. All he could do was shake his head.

*** *** *** *** ***

The Taurus .45 was on the table in front of him as he sat in his boxer shorts in the recliner, smoking a cigarette. He'd spent a good hour beating that pussy up and for some reason he still couldn't sleep so he'd come out to the living room to smoke a cigarette. He brought it up to his lips, took a deep hit off of it and then he exhaled the smoke, blowing smoke rings in the air right in front of him.

'Damn that bitch had some good pussy,' he thought once again as he polished off the rest of the cigarette. He thought about raiding her refrigerator before trying to sleep again, but just as that thought came he heard a knock at the door. *'Now who the fuck could that be?'* He thought.

One part of him was thinking maybe he should go wake Keisha up and let her answer the door. But she had told him didn't no nigga live with her, so he wasn't thinking that. She had said that the babysitter might bring the kids home tonight, so he stood up by the time the second knock came and for a moment his eyes went to the .45 on the table. *'Might be the kids, ain't no sense in scaring them by answering the door in my boxers with a gun,'* he thought and moved over to the door. There was a third knock as he once again glanced back at the gun but didn't grab it.

Rich reached out, unlocked the door and then he pulled it open. His eyes opened wide as he looked straight into B' Nice's face. He saw the fire spit out of the 9mm one time as the slug went into his chest, then he heard the gun spit two more times.

B' Nice stood there and watched as Rich brought his hand up and felt his chest. It was as if he didn't believe he'd really been shot, but the blood poured out like water. His body still stood there in shock and for a minute B' Nice thought that he would have to unload the clip into the nigga. But then it seem to set in on him and his body crumbled to the floor in the door way. B' Nice was about to leave when he heard a noise and looked up to see Keisha in a loose house coat, extremely naked under it. She was standing in the hallway looking at him, but she wasn't scared.

"Oh and tell Chalice it was nice doing business with him," Keisha said.

"You good wit' this? Or do you need us to move the body?" B' Nice asked.

"Child please, I'm about to call the cops," she laughed. "I've already cleaned the niggas pockets. Plus, I've got the five grand Chalice gave me. But look, y'all need to go, I can't wait too late to report this," she finished.

B' Nice tilted his head in respect as he stepped back out of the doorway. He made his way back to the Hummer then pulled the door open to hop inside.

"What's up? You good?" Paris asked from behind the wheel.

"Yeah, yeah. It's all good. Come on let's get to the motel," B' Nice said.

"Aye, I saw some funny shit back in the projects," Que said. He explained to them about the crack head who'd been going around collecting money out of all the pockets of the people they killed and how she was singing praise the black man's God.

"Yo, y'all niggas ain't seen her?" He asked.

"I think I might have saw her," John-John replied.

"I saw her on that back street, back where small world is," B' Nice said.

But Paris started the Hummer, put it into drive and then he pulled off.

"What about you P?" Que asked.

"I gave her the first two hundred dollars and told her to leave that shit alone," he said. "Sounds like she's about to come up."

Trai'Quan

Chapter Fifteen

Chalice already knew where Rugar and his crew would be, mostly because he'd spent a good deal of time studying this nigga's habits. He had also put one of the little trackers that the white guy who sold them the guns gave him, on Rugar's ride. He knew the nigga was in this house and with all the other cars parked there, he guessed his crew was also inside.

The first thing Chalice and Erica did, was flatten all the tires and then they both crept silently around the house. Since it was past nightfall, it was quiet except for the music playing on the inside of the house. Chalice held Erica's hand as he led the way, but she carried the shot gun in her other hand and he had the Black Rain in his.

Coming up to one of the windows where the lights were shining from inside, Chalice held a finger up to his lips. He slowly peeped into the window from an angle. There were four of them inside. One he knew for sure, was the nigga Rugar, but the other three he didn't know. He turned back to Erica and pointed to her, then to the front of the house. Next, he pointed to himself, then to the back of the house. Erica nodded her head that she understood.

He knew that once inside they would both have to hold their own, it was simply a matter of trusting her to be careful. But he knew that she could handle her shit, so he brushed it to the side.

*** *** *** *** ***

"Tommy, it's your bet. Come on nigga, quit stalling," one nigga said.

The one named Tommy Bird puffed on his Black and Mild cigar and mean mugged the nigga from across the table. He picked up a hand full of chips and placed his bet

130

anyway. He held a full house, Ace high, which was a change from all the bullshit he'd been getting.

"I call," Rugar said.

One by one they began to lay their hands out. The full house Ace high won, but didn't anyone get upset about it. Rugar had been winning everybody's money beforehand, so what if his luck gave out. Maybe now they could get some money too.

"Alright Roe, deal the next one. Everybody up?" Tommy asked.

But just as Roe began to shuffle the cards, the back door came open with a loud crash. Everyone was in shock, everyone except Rugar. By the time the door came open and the bullets started to fly, Rugar had jumped through a glass window.

Chalice saw the nigga bolt about the same time that the door opened. *'Damn, not again,'* he thought, referring to having to chase the guy. But he couldn't just up and leave Erica here, alone with these three niggas. Everything was in chaos, movement everywhere. Somebody had even flipped the table onto its side and he thought at least two of them were behind it, shooting.

Erica stood at the edge of the doorway, swinging the shot gun from side to side and letting off a shell every so often.

Kha'chinck..., Boom! Kha'chinck..., Boom!

He saw another nigga run into the next room, but when Chalice took aim and shot the AR-15, he missed and took a chunk out of the wall. He looked once again and saw that Erica had the other two pinned down, so he made his mind up to go after the two on foot. The one he wanted was probably a couple of blocks away by now, so he ran after the nigga who went into the next room.

Erica, with each shot, took away a piece of the table. But she knew the Mossberg was about empty and didn't

131

think she would have time to re-load it. On one of her shots she heard someone cry out. Must've been hit. She pumped her last three shells into the same area of the table and when the shot gun was empty she dropped it and pulled out both 9mms.

Just when she thought she had the upper hand, one of them made a desperate brake and ran out the back door. *'Damn! Again,'* she thought as she rushed into the room with both 9's out in front of her. Cautiously approaching the table, she looked around it and saw one of the niggas lying there, breathing heavy. She also noticed where the shotgun shell had entered his shoulder. Aiming one of her 9's at the dude, she pumped four more slugs into his face and chest area. She turned and did what she knew she had to do next, Erica followed the nigga who ran out the back door.

Chalice moved through the house checking room after room. He found the nigga in one of the back bedrooms, trying to lift a window to climb out. For some reason he seemed to be having trouble, but when Chalice came through the door, he suddenly turned and started to unload the .38 revolver he held. By Grace, there were only three shots and two of them hit Chalice dead center in the chest, throwing his body back into the wall. But because of the vest, it didn't do any serious damage.

When the gun clicked, the nigga looked down into his hand then aimed again and clicked two more times.

Chalice caught his breath and adjusted to the pain in his chest. He watched as the nigga jumped behind the bed. *'Bad move nigga,'* he thought as he lifted both arms, holding both Eagles. He stepped around the edge of the bed and caught the nigga on the floor with the cylinder of the .38 out. The gun wasn't empty but the cylinder just wouldn't turn to the next chamber and the next bullet. What had caused it Chalice didn't know, but he took the opportunity, aimed and squeezed the triggers of both .44's and then watched the nigga's body jerk.

He stopped shooting and stood there listening. There weren't any other shots being fired from the house, but then he heard three shots from outside and they weren't shotgun shots. *'Damn. She must've had one run too,'* he thought. Chalice ran over to the window and used one of his guns to break it. He was thinking that nigga Rugar had a three or four minute lead and wondered if he could still catch him.

Still in thought, he climbed out the window and saw two people running up the street. They were both headed towards a small softball field and he was about to assume one was Erica, when she came up behind him.

"Come on! I've got these niggas on the run!" She told him, but didn't stop.

*** *** *** *** ***

Rugar decided that it was real reckless, him running with Roe Dogg. Even if they both did have guns. He pushed off when he got to the other side of the field and let Roe Dogg pick his own direction. When he turned right, Rugar went to the left. He didn't even look to see if Roe Dogg noticed the move, he was breathing too hard and thinking about living. Now he wished that he hadn't smoked all of those cigarettes and blunts all of his life.

He ran damn near a whole block when he saw the soda company up ahead of him. In his mind he was thinking that he might be able to lose this nigga. He'd been cursing and double cursing himself ever since this nigga busted through the back door. It was all his fault, he should have unloaded his clip into the nigga when he first shot him, made sure that he was dead back then. Now, here it was a year later and this nigga was on his ass like a fly on shit.

As he came closer to the building, Rugar clutched his Glock, praying that he got just one good chance to dome call this nigga. When he reached the fence, he aimed the Glock at the padlock and pulled the trigger. The lock broke so he pulled the fence open and ran inside. At the building, he shot the lock on the large sliding door and then lifted it up about three feet. He got down on his belly, rolled under it and then on the other side, he pulled the door back down.

When he turned and looked around, he saw some machines and stacks, upon stacks of different types of sodas. They almost reached the ceiling. "Gotta find somewhere to hide," he chanted. He was almost out of breath, but Rugar didn't let that stop him, he moved through the building until he came to a line of bottles on the far wall, stacked high. He made his mind up after a quick glance around, then he squeezed between the bottles and the wall itself and prayed.

*** *** *** *** ***

Roe Dogg came up on the gym where he found the door already unlocked. Thinking some kids had been playing in it, he didn't even hesitate to go inside. He knew that one of them was behind him, which one he didn't know, he just hoped it wasn't that crazy bitch with the shotgun. It didn't matter, he was going to hide anyway. Using all of his common sense, Roe ran up the stairs to the bleachers and about half way to the top, he sank down and slid under a set directly in the middle.

*** *** *** *** ***

He heard the two shots a few paces back, but Chalice didn't know what it had been for. Then as he came upon the fence going into the soda company and saw the lock and realized what had happen. He pushed through the fence and walked over to the building. At first he wasn't sure if the nigga had gone into the building or not. But then he saw another broken lock and he knew. *'This nigga's either real stupid, or he's trying to set me up,'* Chalice thought. It didn't matter, he pulled the door up and went inside anyway. This beef was just too personal for him to let this nigga wiggle out of it.

Once inside and still holding both guns in his hand, Chalice began to look around carefully. After a good look, he made up his mind that there weren't a whole lot of places for anybody to hide. The only thing he had to do was figure out where this nigga was hiding. He by passed the soda's that were stacked up to the ceiling but his mind wasn't focused on them. Instead, he was paying attention to the factory machines. They seemed like the most likely place, that is, when he considered the hiding spots.

He tried to move as silently as he could and keep his eyes sharp. For some reason Chalice's hair on the back of his neck stood up. He was having that feeling you get when someone is watching you. He paused a moment and looked around one more time. He still didn't see anything. Not anything that stood out to him.

He'd almost made it to the pouring machine when he got the feeling again. He was no more than three steps away from it when he flinched at the first shot. The shot had come from behind him. Chalice spun around and took aim but before he could pin point the source, another shot came. This one went through his upper right side shoulder. There was a sharp pain that went through his body and then, before he could do anything, there was another shot. This one hit the wall right behind his head. He slipped and fell right in front of a stack of sodas and it was while he was in the process of trying to stand again, that he saw the nigga's feet behind the stack.

*** *** *** *** ***

Erica knew that nigga was somewhere inside this gym, she just had to figure out where. She checked the office and the equipment room but there was no sign of him. She'd even looked in the bathrooms and didn't find him there either. The only thing that was left to check was the bleachers and there was a long set of them. She figured to go all the way to the top and work her way down. If she didn't find the nigga by then, well fuck it.

That's exactly what she did and it was as she descended the steps from the top, that she saw the nigga. He'd been lying down between the bleachers almost at the top. "Damn nigga, what you gone do, die like a punk?" She asked.

Roe looked up at her as she stood there, holding her two guns and looking like Pam Grier in Foxy Comes to Harlem. He couldn't help it, his pride got the best of him. "Oh, so you a bad bitch since you done caught a nigga down hard. Well go ahead and shoot then, you don't get no points for killin a nigga like this."

Erica shook her head. Then told him, "Nigga, Kenya ain't the badest bitch from Miami. She got that shit from me and just to show you how bad a bitch I am Nigga, fuck yo points!" She aimed both guns at him and squeezed both triggers at the same time. Erica watched as the slugs from both her guns ate his face.

*** *** *** *** ***

When the pain subsided in his shoulder, Chalice stood up and raised both pistols. He took aim at the bottom of the stack of sodas and started shooting. Standing there, he watched as the tower of bottles shattered and collapsed into a pile.

"Oh shit! Oh shit..., help! Somebody help me!"

Chalice heard the nigga crying out and made his way

136

over to the pile up. Soda was all over the floor and his feet squished through it with each step he took. When he reached the area where he heard the nigga crying from, he looked down and saw that the nigga was covered in glass and soda. The closer he looked he noticed that there was blood mixed with the liquid and he saw cuts on the niggas face.

"Man look…, I'm sorry. It was all that nigga Rich's idea to rob y'all. The nigga called me up and I didn't even know you or the broad," Rugar plead.

"Oh yeah. Nigga you threatened me at the store. I'm quite sure you watched the joint before you robbed us. You must've thought I was lame," Chalice said.

"N...nah... man. A nigga was down bad bruh. I was just trying to eat. Damn nigga, don't you respect the streets?" Rugar asked.

Chalice raised the .44 Desert Eagles and pointed them at the nigga.

"Hold up nigga.... I just told you the truth!" Rugar cried.

"Yeah," Chalice agreed. "And the truth shall set you free. Oh and yeah..., just so you know, me, respect the streets? Nigga, I am the streets!" He then unloaded the rest of the two clips into the nigga's body.

When the hammer kicked back to let him know the guns were empty, Chalice's shoulders dropped and he took a deep breath. It was all over now…, or was it....

Chapter Sixteen

"**Turn the lights down low, tell me what you see. Yeah, tell me what you know, bout everything you and me, baby if you wanna go then I gotta place we could be, lady.... baby....**"
-Maxwell, Now 2001 w/as my girl

10 Months later

The chief still couldn't figure it out. They had a slew of unsolved murder cases and the so-called Four Horsemen had vanished, like thieves in the night. One thing was for sure, they had wiped out about half of the cities drug dealers and damn near killed every swinging dick in the Southside projects.

Then there was the 'born again' crackhead, Kenya. She'd been telling everybody that she met the Black God in the flesh on that 'Day of Judgement.' She'd stopped smoking crack and came up with a good deal of money.

Now days, Kenya wasn't crackhead Kenya. Now she was the woman who sold the weed. Rumor was that she found $80,000 that night. Now her teeth were fixed, she had both ivory and gold teeth to replace the ones she'd lost. Her weight was back. At 5'4 she was now 145lbs with her body measurements being around 35-25-40 and she had a house on 8th and Grand. A house that another woman moved out of because one of the dope boys was gunned down in her living room. She said the house had a ghost.

Chief Washington thought, and it wasn't the half of it, that there was a war brewing. The streets were buzzing loud about some Miami drug Kingpin named Big Afrika. They said he'd just arrived in Augusta two months ago but he hadn't done anything. Then there was the tension between Mustafa out in Barton Village and this guy Paris. That was big. In fact, it was real big. They were, according to the snitches, playing war games. Killing one another's workers and sending their bodies back to each other.

Then there was Cory from Sand Hills who was bumping heads with this guy B' Nice. Those two were at war over who would control the Hill.

Chief Washington sighed, he had a lot of problems and not one good solution. On top of all that garbage, he had to deal with Internal Affairs, who had just made their presence known. It seemed that he had a group of crooked cops who were part of this local crime family, calling its self 'Black Ayla.' An Arabic word, Ayla meant "family," and he'd just found out who was supposed to be this 'black family.'

Chief Washington looked down at the file lying on his desk. On top of the file were season tickets for four to the Augusta Masters, a gift from the guy whose face looked up at him from the picture on the folder. They called him Chalice.... Chalice Black....

To Be Continued...
Extended Clip 2
Coming Soon

Submission Guideline

Submit the first three chapters of your completed manuscript to ldpsubmissions@gmail.com, subject line: Your book's title. The manuscript must be in a .doc file and sent as an attachment. Document should be in Times New Roman, double spaced and in size 12 font. Also, provide your synopsis and full contact information. If sending multiple submissions, they must each be in a separate email.

Have a story but no way to send it electronically? You can still submit to LDP/Ca$h Presents. Send in the first three chapters, written or typed, of your completed manuscript to:

**LDP: Submissions Dept
Po Box 944
Stockbridge, Ga 30281**

DO NOT send original manuscript. Must be a duplicate.

Provide your synopsis and a cover letter containing your full contact information.

Thanks for considering LDP and Ca$h Presents.

Trai'Quan

BOW DOWN TO MY GANGSTA

By **Ca$h**

TORN BETWEEN TWO

By **Coffee**

THE STREETS STAINED MY SOUL **II**

By **Marcellus Allen**

BLOOD OF A BOSS **VI**

SHADOWS OF THE GAME II

By **Askari**

LOYAL TO THE GAME **IV**

By **T.J. & Jelissa**

IF LOVING YOU IS WRONG… **III**

By **Jelissa**

TRUE SAVAGE **VIII**

MIDNIGHT CARTEL III

DOPE BOY MAGIC IV

CITY OF KINGZ II

By **Chris Green**

BLAST FOR ME **III**

A SAVAGE DOPEBOY III

CUTTHROAT MAFIA III

DUFFLE BAG CARTEL VI

By **Ghost**

A HUSTLER'S DECEIT III

KILL ZONE **II**

BAE BELONGS TO ME III

Trai'Quan

By Troublesome

YAYO IV

GHOST MOB

Stilloan Robinson

KINGPIN DREAMS III

By Paper Boi Rari

CREAM II

By Yolanda Moore

SON OF A DOPE FIEND III

By Renta

FOREVER GANGSTA II

GLOCKS ON SATIN SHEETS III

By Adrian Dulan

LOYALTY AIN'T PROMISED III

By Keith Williams

THE PRICE YOU PAY FOR LOVE II

By Destiny Skai

CONFESSIONS OF A GANGSTA III

By Nicholas Lock

I'M NOTHING WITHOUT HIS LOVE II

SINS OF A THUG II

By Monet Dragun

LIFE OF A SAVAGE IV

MURDA SEASON IV

GANGLAND CARTEL III

By **Romell Tukes**

QUIET MONEY IV

THUG LIFE II

Extended Clip

EXTENDED CLIP II

By **Trai'Quan**

THE STREETS MADE ME III

By **Larry D. Wright**

THE ULTIMATE SACRIFICE VI

IF YOU CROSS ME ONCE II

ANGEL III

By **Anthony Fields**

FRIEND OR FOE III

By **Mimi**

SAVAGE STORMS II

By **Meesha**

BLOOD ON THE MONEY III

By J-Blunt

THE STREETS WILL NEVER CLOSE II

By K'ajji

NIGHTMARES OF A HUSTLA III

By King Dream

THE WIFEY I USED TO BE II

By Nicole Goosby

IN THE ARM OF HIS BOSS

By Jamila

MONEY, MURDER & MEMORIES II

Malik D. Rice

<u>Available Now</u>

RESTRAINING ORDER **I & II**

Trai'Quan

By **CA$H & Coffee**

LOVE KNOWS NO BOUNDARIES **I II & III**

By **Coffee**

RAISED AS A GOON I, II, III & IV

BRED BY THE SLUMS I, II, III

BLAST FOR ME I & II

ROTTEN TO THE CORE I II III

A BRONX TALE I, II, III

DUFFLE BAG CARTEL I II III IV V

HEARTLESS GOON I II III IV

A SAVAGE DOPEBOY I II

HEARTLESS GOON I II III

DRUG LORDS I II III

CUTTHROAT MAFIA I II

By **Ghost**

LAY IT DOWN **I & II**

LAST OF A DYING BREED

BLOOD STAINS OF A SHOTTA I & II III

By **Jamaica**

LOYAL TO THE GAME I II III

LIFE OF SIN I, II III

By **TJ & Jelissa**

BLOODY COMMAS I & II

SKI MASK CARTEL I II & III

KING OF NEW YORK I II,III IV V

RISE TO POWER I II III

COKE KINGS I II III IV

BORN HEARTLESS I II III IV

145

Extended Clip

KING OF THE TRAP

By **T.J. Edwards**

IF LOVING HIM IS WRONG...I & II

LOVE ME EVEN WHEN IT HURTS I II III

By **Jelissa**

WHEN THE STREETS CLAP BACK I & II III

THE HEART OF A SAVAGE I II

By **Jibril Williams**

A DISTINGUISHED THUG STOLE MY HEART I II & III

LOVE SHOULDN'T HURT I II III IV

RENEGADE BOYS I II III IV

PAID IN KARMA I II III

SAVAGE STORMS

By **Meesha**

A GANGSTER'S CODE I &, II III

A GANGSTER'S SYN I II III

THE SAVAGE LIFE I II III

CHAINED TO THE STREETS I II III

BLOOD ON THE MONEY I II

By J-Blunt

PUSH IT TO THE LIMIT

By **Bre' Hayes**

BLOOD OF A BOSS **I, II, III, IV, V**

SHADOWS OF THE GAME

By **Askari**

THE STREETS BLEED MURDER **I, II & III**

THE HEART OF A GANGSTA I II& III

By **Jerry Jackson**

147

Extended Clip

DOPE BOY MAGIC I, II, III

MIDNIGHT CARTEL I II

CITY OF KINGZ

By **Chris Green**

A DOPEBOY'S PRAYER

By **Eddie "Wolf" Lee**

THE KING CARTEL **I, II & III**

By **Frank Gresham**

THESE NIGGAS AIN'T LOYAL **I, II & III**

By **Nikki Tee**

GANGSTA SHYT **I II &III**

By **CATO**

THE ULTIMATE BETRAYAL

By **Phoenix**

BOSS'N UP **I , II & III**

By **Royal Nicole**

I LOVE YOU TO DEATH

By Destiny J

I RIDE FOR MY HITTA

I STILL RIDE FOR MY HITTA

By **Misty Holt**

LOVE & CHASIN' PAPER

By **Qay Crockett**

TO DIE IN VAIN

SINS OF A HUSTLA

By **ASAD**

BROOKLYN HUSTLAZ

By **Boogsy Morina**

Trai'Quan

BROOKLYN ON LOCK I & II

By **Sonovia**

GANGSTA CITY

By **Teddy Duke**

A DRUG KING AND HIS DIAMOND I & II III

A DOPEMAN'S RICHES

HER MAN, MINE'S TOO I, II

CASH MONEY HO'S

THE WIFEY I USED TO BE

By Nicole Goosby

TRAPHOUSE KING **I II & III**

KINGPIN KILLAZ I II III

STREET KINGS I II

PAID IN BLOOD **I II**

CARTEL KILLAZ I II III

DOPE GODS I II

By **Hood Rich**

LIPSTICK KILLAH **I, II, III**

CRIME OF PASSION I II & III

FRIEND OR FOE I II

By **Mimi**

STEADY MOBBN' **I, II, III**

THE STREETS STAINED MY SOUL

By **Marcellus Allen**

WHO SHOT YA **I, II, III**

SON OF A DOPE FIEND I II

Renta

GORILLAZ IN THE BAY **I II III IV**

Extended Clip

TEARS OF A GANGSTA I II

3X KRAZY

DE'KARI

TRIGGADALE I II III

Elijah R. Freeman

GOD BLESS THE TRAPPERS I, II, III

THESE SCANDALOUS STREETS I, II, III

FEAR MY GANGSTA I, II, III IV, V

THESE STREETS DON'T LOVE NOBODY I, II

BURY ME A G I, II, III, IV, V

A GANGSTA'S EMPIRE I, II, III, IV

THE DOPEMAN'S BODYGAURD I II

THE REALEST KILLAZ I II III

Tranay Adams

THE STREETS ARE CALLING

Duquie Wilson

MARRIED TO A BOSS… I II III

By Destiny Skai & Chris Green

KINGZ OF THE GAME I II III IV V

Playa Ray

SLAUGHTER GANG I II III

RUTHLESS HEART I II III

By Willie Slaughter

FUK SHYT

By Blakk Diamond

DON'T F#CK WITH MY HEART I II

By Linnea

ADDICTED TO THE DRAMA I II III

Extended Clip

By **Romell Tukes**

LOYALTY AIN'T PROMISED I II

By Keith Williams

QUIET MONEY I II III

THUG LIFE

EXTENDED CLIP

By **Trai'Quan**

THE STREETS MADE ME I II

By **Larry D. Wright**

THE ULTIMATE SACRIFICE I, II, III, IV, V

KHADIFI

IF YOU CROSS ME ONCE

ANGEL I II

By **Anthony Fields**

THE LIFE OF A HOOD STAR

By Ca$h & Rashia Wilson

THE STREETS WILL NEVER CLOSE

By K'ajji

CREAM

By Yolanda Moore

NIGHTMARES OF A HUSTLA I II

By King Dream

<u>BOOKS BY LDP'S CEO, CA$H</u>

<u>TRUST IN NO MAN</u>

<u>TRUST IN NO MAN 2</u>

<u>TRUST IN NO MAN 3</u>

<u>BONDED BY BLOOD</u>

<u>SHORTY GOT A THUG</u>

<u>THUGS CRY</u>

<u>THUGS CRY 2</u>

<u>THUGS CRY 3</u>

<u>TRUST NO BITCH</u>

<u>TRUST NO BITCH 2</u>

<u>TRUST NO BITCH 3</u>

<u>TIL MY CASKET DROPS</u>

<u>RESTRAINING ORDER</u>

<u>RESTRAINING ORDER 2</u>

<u>IN LOVE WITH A CONVICT</u>

<u>LIFE OF A HOOD STAR</u>

Extended Clip